Frankie B
a spell in paradise

AF072945

ANDIE LOW

Squabbling Sparrows Press

All names, characters, places, and incidents in this publication are fictitious or are used fictitiously. Any resemblance to real persons, living or dead, events or locales is entirely coincidental.

© Andrene Low 2020

All rights reserved. No part of this text may be reproduced or transmitted in any form or by any means, including photocopying, recording, or other electronic or mechanical methods, without the express written permission of the author or publisher, except in the case of brief quotations embodied in critical reviews and certain other non-commercial uses permitted by copyright law.

For information regarding permission, email the author at andrenelow@andrenelowauthor.com, subject line: Permission

ISBN: 978-0-9951388-5-8

1

Frankie sniffs the air. Nope, she can't detect a hint of snow. Wow, she's really done it; she's magically transported her schooner, the *Pearl*, from Seattle to *Garnet Cove* in the Caribbean without the need for sick bags. This is definitely a first and makes a welcome change.

She puts the smooth trip down to her new powers courtesy of the energy meld with Zane and the three vampires on board. Well, that and the gorgeous silver wand Zane, her merman boyfriend, gave her on Valentine's Day.

"You can get up now, Dex. We're here."

"We are?" The Jack Russell keeps his head jammed under a pillow, paws atop, holding it down.

"Yep, we sure are." Frankie swings her legs over the side of the bed, and stands. A casual wave of her wand and she's better dressed to suit the local temperatures. No point being wrapped up for a Seattle winter when you're in the tropics. She's in shorts and a tank top and wearing a pair of silver sandals rather than her standard-issue boots.

Another wave of her wand and she's even a little tanned. No need for everyone to have to wear sunglasses due to her winter whiteness. The spell is also designed to protect her from sunburn and help her blend in. Not an easy thing with her fiery red hair.

"Come on, up you get ya lazy pup. We've got good guys to rescue."

Frankie's out in the corridor that leads to the other cabins before Dex catches up with her. His eyes all squinty, says he's still unable to believe they've arrived, at least not without the return of their last meal.

Frankie walks up and down the corridor knocking on doors and yelling out that they can put away their sick bags. She's a touch miffed when Magda, Sophie and Zane are as incredulous as Dex at the nausea-free trip. Dominik and Luca, the two male vampires don't comment. No doubt this is down to it being their first trip with Frankie at the helm.

"Hey, if you guys don't believe me, get up on deck." Frankie doesn't bother traipsing along the corridor and up the circular staircase that leads topside. Instead she waves her wand around herself and Dex, leaving the others to follow. It'll also give the non-magical vampires and Nana Peg, her shifter relation, a chance to change into something cooler.

To be fair though, for Nana Peg to change into something cooler would involve a visit to a doggie day spa. Due to a spell Frankie had put on the portal to the Wereall's home, her nana is stuck here and in her animal form. Frankie's best description of this is a dog walking like a woman, and yet not. The tail her nana sports when she's annoyed is more feline than anything Dex would be happy with.

On seeing where they are, Frankie wrinkles her brow. They're not sitting alongside the *Jolly Roger* her granddad's launch, at the back of the island as planned. Nope, they're bang up against the dock that bisects the bay in front of the resort. Hah, so much for a stealthy arrival.

Frankie doesn't waste time wondering why this is. She points her wand at the stern and then the bow. She then stabs it toward both the port and starboard sides of the vessel. All of this is completed while muttering an incantation under her breath. The vessel flickers for a second before looking as it had before.

The difference is the boat, and everyone on it, is invisible to all but themselves. The ward is also designed to conceal them once they disembark. The one unknown is whether she's managed to have them blinking out of sight before they've been spotted. At most the *Pearl's* brief appearance will be put down to hangovers. The sun just making an appearance over the horizon, she knows it's crazy early, so at least this much has gone to plan.

Frankie's scanning the resort with the vintage brass telescope from the helm when she's joined by Zane and Sophie. The pair arriving ahead of the others is to be expected with the witch and merman/warlock hybrid able to magic up summer clothes as easily as Frankie herself.

Zane looks down the dock toward the resort. "I thought we agreed we should arrive around the back of the island."

Frankie takes the telescope away from her eye and huffs. Not at Zane, but at her powers once again proving unpredictable. Her getting the boat here so easily had her thinking things were finally turning around, but apparently not.

"Yeah, that was the plan. Apparently my powers had different ideas. I've already cloaked us and it doesn't appear as though we've been spotted."

"Mind if I have a look?" Zane holds his hand out and, after having another quick scan of the resort, Frankie hands him the telescope.

While she could tell him the place looks deserted, she knows it's easier, and quicker, that he discover this for himself. Even though he trusts her implicitly, there are some male traits she's never going to beat out of him. He can be as bad as her dad in this regard.

Thank goodness Colin had decided to stay behind in Seattle. He'd be bombarding her with 'helpful' suggestions by now, the sort that result in her left eye twitching.

Just like last time Frankie was here, the dock is empty, apart from the *Pearl* and a small inflatable craft that's seen better days. If the patches are any indicator, the last thing to use the small boat was a porcupine. This is such a far cry from earlier visits, when the dock had been jammed with million dollar yachts and cruisers. No doubt word of the island being haunted has made it back to the mainland, scaring away any new visitors.

As empty as the dock, is the resort. The place has a deserted air about it and Frankie doubts them getting closer is going to change this. Despite scanning the telescope back and forth as Zane is doing, she didn't spot a living soul. Apart that is from a couple of guards lying on the beach near the end of the dock.

And, if the island's security force are lying down on the job, this proves there isn't a lot happening. Although how anyone can actually sleep there is beyond Frankie. As early as it is, the humidity has to be edging toward one hundred percent. She runs her hands down her arms to quell the prickling sensation this has resulted in.

The three vampires make their way up on deck and Frankie can't help but smirk at Dominik's ensemble. When she'd put together their outfits, she'd done so with resort-wear in mind. It's this that has Dominik in yellow shorts and a shirt that's heavy on the pineapples.

That he's not happy with her choice is obvious by his expression. His frown turns to downright annoyance when he spots what Zane is wearing. Rather than channel his inner Ken doll, the Nautilus is wearing khaki cargo shorts and a white t-shirt.

The shirt is tight and shows every dip and curve of the merman's chest. It's enough to have Frankie licking her lips. Instead of golden leather sandals like Dominik's wearing, Zane's in battered boat shoes.

The comparison between the two alpha males is giggle-worthy, although Frankie squelches hers. No point getting the pair at odds with each other this early in the piece. Frankie waves her wand in Dominik's direction, leaving him dressed similarly to Zane. The colors however are very different to avoid them looking like twins. She doubts either male would be happy with this.

A second wave of her wand and Magda and Luca are also more appropriately dressed. There being no tourists at the resort, the need to hide in plain sight is moot. And to be fair this won't be necessary if the camouflage spell holds. Frankie is confident it will and so they may as well be comfortable.

A change of wardrobe won't do much good for Nana Peg. Unless Frankie does something about it, the poor woman will be up for dying from heat exhaustion. Even Dex is suffering from too much hair.

Frankie thinks about it for just a beat. She waves her wand first at Dex and then Nana Peg, treating them to the doggy day spa equivalent of a Brazilian. While Dex's response is to cheer telepathically, Nana Peg squeals in horror. Her hands race to cover strategic body parts, showing she feels naked thanks to the 'short, back and sides' Frankie's hit her with. It's this very touching of her body that reminds the shifter that she's wearing a kaftan. She acknowledges Frankie's haircut with a brief nod of thanks.

This is as much as she ever gets out of her Nana Peg. The woman is the proverbial closed book and as much a stranger as when she'd first followed Frankie home. Frankie's tried striking up conversations to find out more about her ancestry, for all the good it's done her. Nana Peg is queen of the monosyllabic response, taking self-effacement to a whole new level. It's something Frankie finds incredibly frustrating. Not that she's given up, just yet.

Everyone sorted; Frankie waves her wand in

the direction of her own feet, swapping her silver sandals for beaten-up sneakers. There's one thing left to do before they step onto the dock.

Frankie looks to Zane, knowing he's more than powerful enough to conceal the group. Sure she's already included them in the cloaking spell, but the risk is still too great that something will go pear-shaped. The reliability of her magic, while getting better, isn't there yet. It's one thing for the boat to pop into view; it's another for them to appear out of nowhere, especially in hostile territory.

Frankie waits until Zane is looking at her before speaking. "You wanna do the honors?"

Rather than respond verbally, he waves his wand around the whole group.

If Frankie wasn't watching carefully, she'd not have noticed any difference. As it is, she's able to see the slight glow that surrounds each member of the team. It's this spell that will allow them to see each other, but mean they're invisible to everyone else. On top of this, the group can also talk normally without being overhead. And, if this wasn't enough, they're also sniff-proof.

All of this had been decided in their planning session at *Magic Beans,* the café near the home of the Marina Coven. It was her Nana Peg who'd suggested masking their body odor. It isn't that any of them are in need of deodorant. Heck, even Dex is freshly washed. The problem is that the

Wereall's sense of smell is three times that of a domestic dog.

Frankie suspects, if it hadn't been for an off-shore breeze, if there were any shifters around they'd have been detected by now. Technically with her freezing the only portal on the island, there shouldn't be any Wereall in residence. But never say never, especially where her magic is concerned. This was another reason she wanted to arrive around the back of the island.

Meanwhile the concealment spell will allow them to move around the resort without worrying about being spotted, heard or smelled. Even if anyone is alerted to their presence, they'll have no way of keeping tabs on them.

Frankie's the last to jump off the *Pearl* and onto the dock. The expressions on the faces of the team, lets her know something is up. Yep, sure enough on turning, she finds the *Pearl*, or rather she doesn't.

"Jinxed jackrabbits, I didn't mean for that to happen."

The boat was supposed to still be visible to anyone who'd been aboard when she put the cloaking spell in place. This isn't the case.

Zane slings his arm around her shoulders and gives her a tight squeeze. "You may as well leave it as it is. We'll still be able to find it."

He's got a point. Frankie could really mess things up if she plays around with the spell now.

Better to leave it well alone. Not that she can leave the boat where it is. While the *Pearl* is invisible, the gap in the water where the hull displaces the seawater isn't. It's this that sees her slide the *Pearl* away from the dock by thirty feet or so.

The schooner taken care of, they can get back on track with the plan they'd hashed out at *Magic Beans*. Frankie shoves the eyeglass into her backpack, and takes a few steps along the dock toward the resort. She then stops. Turning to face the others, she holds her hand up.

"Hang on a second. Before we go any further, just let me check on something." Without waiting for a response, she transports herself to the open space she knows of at the very top of the island.

It's this vantage point that will allow her to see if her granddad's launch is still sitting where it had been last time she visited the island. It might be because the *Jolly Roger* is no longer there that the *Pearl* materialized out front of the resort. Part of Frankie hopes this is true. Better this than being lumbered with unreliable powers and with the task ahead, her magical abilities need to be rock solid.

Frankie has no need of the telescope to note there aren't any vessels anchored at the back of the island. Unless, that is, you know where and what to look for.

A rough idea of where the boat should be means she finds the hull-shaped gap in the water quickly. It's the potential presence of her relations that was her other reason for wanting to materialize at the back of the island. Far better to know what those two are up to than not.

Unfortunately because of the concealment spell she's not able to tell if Anne and Calico Jack are actually on board the launch. As there's no point in continuing to stare at the space occupied by the vessel, she transports herself back down to the dock to join the others.

"They're anchored where I thought they'd be." She has no need to explain who it is she's talking about. The larcenous pair still skulking around the island looking for more treasure featured often in their planning sessions.

"Okay, let's do this." Zane puts his arm possessively around Frankie's shoulders and together they walk down the dock toward the resort. Frankie basks in the warm glow of Zane's affection, even if she knows its main purpose is to have Dominik backing off.

On hearing muttering from behind her, she knows the message has been received loud and clear. Thankfully as they get closer to the sleeping guards, the vampire quits his whining. The other thing that quiets is the footsteps of the team with everyone placing their feet carefully. The camouflage ward means there's no need, but it's a hard habit to break.

Even Dex is trying his best to stop his toenails

from clattering on the wooden boards. Sophie's hamster familiar, Stinky, has disappeared right inside the witch's backpack, no doubt worried she's squeaking too loudly. "Guys, there's no need for all this *Pink Panther* action. They can't hear us." Frankie's voice sounds loud, even to her own ears.

As tempting as it is to go straight to the cliff and the entrance to *All Hallows Keep*, it's not to be. First off is checking out the two guards. They then need to get a handle on what's happening at the resort itself. On the face of it, this appears to be not a lot.

While the prison is run by the Werealls — a shifter race with a tendency to resemble an explosion in a petting zoo — it's the Garnet family who are behind a lot of those wrongfully imprisoned. There's no point in freeing a stack of innocents, if the Garnets are only going to go and lock them up again.

It's this family that's responsible for the death of Frankie's mom, making her animosity toward them understandable. If she can pin Patsy Bonny's murder on one of them, then for sure she's going to do so. Especially given the family had actually been targeting her at the time of the 'accident'.

Despite having taken George Garnet prisoner, she's no closer to discovering which family member is responsible. She would have thought he'd weaken by now; instead he seems to enjoy spending his days in the coven leader's terrarium. Perhaps it's the heat lamps and live cockroaches on tap that have him smiling that little gecko smile of his? She's starting to think he really doesn't know who did it.

As they near the end of the dock a few things become apparent. The guards aren't snoring as would be usual for men this large sleeping on their backs. They're not even asleep.

Nope, they're pegged out on the beach like some nasty science experiment.

2

Frankie doesn't need to get closer than she already is to know the two guards have left this world. Thanks to her new vampire senses, she can tell they're devoid of all energy. As if this wasn't enough, the bodies have attracted enough flies that they're close to being airborne. No, they're dead and have been for a couple of days at the very least.

Frankie staggers to a standstill and Zane unhooks his arm from around her shoulders. He then slaps one hand over his mouth and walks forward. Dominik, Luca and Magda, who don't need to breathe, tag along. Of some surprise is Nana Peg joins them, a hand firmly clasped over her face like a furry gasmask.

Sophie, Dex and Frankie watch the five of them as they peer down at the bodies. It's Zane who leans forward and removes something from the shirt pocket of the guard on the right. Even as far back as they are, Frankie's able to hear the crinkle of paper.

A second later, Zane waves his wand and the two bodies disappear. On the one hand, Frankie's annoyed as she'd have liked to see if she could spot any clues. On the other hand, she's thankful she doesn't need to look for those very clues.

The bodies disposed of; Frankie, Sophie and Dex join the others, with Frankie holding her hand out toward Zane. "Can I read it?"

He passes the note over to her allowing her to see the paper is greasy and stained. There are even a couple of flies clinging tenaciously to one corner. Frankie yanks her hand back. There is no way she's touching that.

"Can you just hold it so I can read it?"

Zane does so, allowing her and Sophie to scan it together. Not that it's an easy read, with the spidery writing difficult to decipher. Someone obviously went to the same school of calligraphy as Gwen Morris, the coven leader's evil daughter.

One thing that's not difficult to interpret is the threat. Basically if they stay, they'll end up in the same state as the guards. They're still digesting this when Zane leans down and holds the piece of paper low enough that Dex can read it too. This is much easier than them having to bring the small Jack Russell up to speed.

A quick scan of the note and Dex backs away,

his sensitive nose wrinkled in disgust. *"Wow, that's what you call a lousy welcome."*

Zane straightens and Frankie's re-reads the missive. "Yeah, but who's it from. And for that matter, who's it to, because it aint obvious." The only thing that's in no doubt is that whoever wrote it isn't keen on visitors.

Other than themselves and Stanley, no-one knew their final destination. It therefore seems doubtful word has got out about their mission. The only thing not in doubt is that the team has no intention of leaving as instructed.

Everyone having read the 'letter of welcome', Zane waves his wand and the note is safely tucked inside a sealable clear baggie. He slides this into a zippered pocket on his backpack before once again slinging it over his shoulder. "This changes everything."

He's got that right. Even with their ability to sneak around undetected, their arrival will be noticed. The bodies no longer being on the beach positively shrieks to the murderer that someone has arrived.

Frankie looks at the huge stakes still sticking out of the white sand, the flies buzzing around them in confusion. "What did you do with the guards?"

"I sent them back to their people. They won't know how they died, but they will at least be able to mourn their loved ones."

Frankie knows all about the importance of this. She'd faced so many hurdles after the loss of her mom that her own grieving had been put to one side. On some levels she still hasn't dealt with it properly. Perhaps this is down to her helping her dad deal with the sad news?

She wonders how it would have been if she'd had a guy like Zane supporting her, and not the low-life she'd been dating at the time. All he'd done in response to her distress was to whine she was crying too much and bringing him down.

It was why the creep dumped her.

It was also why she swallowed her grief and carried on as if nothing about her life had changed. Well, after she'd burned all his belongings in his front yard, that is.

Now she's come into her powers, perhaps it's time to pay him a little visit? He'd suit being a rat, seeing he is one. As focused as she is on her ex, when Zane puts his arm back around her shoulders, she responds without thinking. This sees him flipped over her shoulder and slammed down on the beach. She jams her foot hard against his throat, holding him in place. This is immediately followed by an abject apology and her helping him to stand again.

The only person amused is Dominik, with him making no attempt to staunch his guffaws despite getting the evil eye from Frankie.

Doing his best to ignore the vampire, Zane

dusts himself free of sand. "What the heck was that all about?" His voice has a wheezy quality to it, no doubt brought on by the rapid emptying of his lungs.

Rather than air her dirty laundry in front of the others, Frankie replies telepathically.

"I'm so sorry, I was thinking about what I'd do to my ex if ever I ran into him."

"Okay. Remind me never to break up with you."

"Not happening, unless you screw up big time."

Zane gives her the side eye, before putting his arm back around her shoulders. This time he's obvious about it and moves slowly in order to avoid another introduction to the beach.

His softly-softly approach reminds Frankie the group's own stealth has been blown sky-high. Question is what do they do about it? While it would be easy to turn tail and head home, this isn't an option for her. It's been months since she broke her dad out of *All Hallows Keep* and he's still not over it. Thoughts of leaving other innocents to suffer the same fate aren't to be borne. It's something she's lost sleep over.

She was starting to think her fixation was unnatural until her Nana Peg took her to one side. It turns out the Wereall are uniquely suited to their role as prison masters. There's something in their DNA that has them able to detect evil in others. Frankie argued she hadn't picked up on Gwen

Morris being evil to the core, or her ex for that matter.

"But that was when you were still under the influence of your mother's jinx," Nana Peg, had quietly explained.

That her nana was up to speed on this told of her and Colin, Frankie's dad, having quite the conflabs when Frankie was out. What else does her Wereall relation know about her?

Leaving her thoughts alone for the moment, Frankie fans her face, hoping to create a small breeze. It's in vain, given the humidity. "We need to regroup, but not out here. It's too blinkin' hot."

"You're right, Shortcake. We should be able to get something cold to drink in the restaurant."

Zane takes his arm away from her shoulders and urges her forward, his large hand hot against the small of her back. Again she knows this, and the use of his pet name for her, are further messages to Dominik to back off.

Luckily, the vampire hasn't been too overt with his passion to claim her, restricting this to seductive smiles and innuendo. Oh, and him brushing past her more often than necessary. The hardest part about the last action is the fizz of excitement this incites in Frankie. Hey, he's a gorgeous looking guy — ah vampire — and she's only human-ish.

The biggest disappointment on entering the restaurant is to find the air-conditioning isn't on.

The other thing that's missing is any solid furniture. Everything in there had been smashed by Magda and Frankie during their last visit to the establishment. Thank the Goddess almost half the team are magical.

In less than five minutes Sophie, Zane and Frankie have replaced all the broken furniture. There's now enough seating for everyone, with even Stinky and Dex having an ottoman apiece. Best of all, Sophie has managed to get the air-con going, and it's blasting the large space with cool air.

In the interim Nana Peg has had a good rummage through all the glass fronted fridges and got cold drinks for everyone, including water for the two familiars. That the fridges are still in action indicates the place hasn't been completely abandoned.

There must be someone from the Garnet family still roaming around. Frankie doubts very much that running the place has been entirely down to George Garnet. He simply doesn't appear bright enough to be up to such a responsibility. His pot stomach when he was human being better suited to heading up Happy Hour than the whole resort. Sunning himself under the heat lamp in the terrarium at Stanley's place is definitely more his style.

Only when everyone is comfortable do they

start to mull over how the change in circumstances will affect their plans.

Frankie puts her soda down on the coffee table in front of the sofa she's sharing with Zane. "Whoever murdered the guards was expecting someone. How did they die, by the way?" She's not being morbid by asking this question of Zane. Rather she wants to get a handle on what sort of adversary they're facing. It might even indicate whether the killer is male or female, human or magical, or even Wereall.

Zane scrunches up his forehead. "I'm not entirely sure. It could have been a combination of things. At the very least a couple of days on the beach without water would be enough. But, whoever it was needed to have been strong enough to overpower the guards in order to peg them out like that."

"Unless they were drugged." So low is Nana Peg's voice that if the Wereall hadn't been in the seat right next to the sofa, Frankie wouldn't have heard her.

Frankie repeats her relation's comment, getting nods of agreement all around. It would be the simplest solution. It would also mean it'd be easy for a woman to have done the deed, although she'd still need to be strong. The pegs used to secure the guards had been as thick as Frankie's forearms. This would make driving them through the uniforms and into the sand a lot harder than pushing in a beach umbrella. And even that could see you packing a mallet along with the sunscreen. Or so she's been told, not being a fan of the beach herself.

Magda, takes her attention away from Luca, her new husband, long enough to join the discussion. "I could not detect the damage." She goes quiet for a second. "On the bodies. No physical 'arm 'ad come to them."

"Other than the whole dying thing, that is." Frankie looks at the energy vamp. She didn't even know Magda was capable of this sort of analysis? Does her having shared energy with the vampires, mean she's capable of this too?

She casts her mind back to when she'd been looking at the two bodies, albeit from a distance. Nope, all she got was an absence of energy and not anything specific the likes of which Magda is talking about. Even Luca is nodding in agreement with his wife. They really do act as a single unit; with this apparent by the blood-tinged sparks of energy currently flying between the pair.

"Hang on, hang on. We're going to need to keep track of this." A brief wave of her hand and Frankie is armed with pen and paper. Opening the small notebook, she writes POTENTIAL KILLERS across the top of the first page. She resists the urge to put little skulls above each 'i', but only just.

"Okay, the most obvious choice is someone

from the Garnet family." She writes their name directly under the heading.

"But these are their guards," says Sophie, while scratching the top of Stinky's head. It's something that gives the hamster a decided punk vibe

Zane takes a sip of his soda before speaking. "They'd consider the guards expendable with the resort apparently empty. They don't strike me as honorable people."

He's got that right, with a lot of prisoners in *All Hallows Keep* guilty of nothing more than being business rivals of the family. These poor souls spend their days as indentured servants, helping run the family's global business interests. Their combined brainpower used like a supercomputer of sorts.

Then there are the magical folk who are locked up because of the she-devil, Mimi Merriweather. Following her seduction of the patriarch of the Garnet Clan, Stanley's ex-wife had gained entrance to *All Hallows Keep*. Once there, she'd made herself irresistible to William, the Commander of the Wereall. This allowed her to help herself to the powers of any new intake of magical prisoners. It was this that had made her almost indestructible.

Almost.

Thanks to mean fighting skills and the knowledge if she lost she'd die, Frankie had wrangled

Mimi into the *Syphonia*. The machine then stripped the Succubus of all her stolen powers. Unfortunately she still had her own.

These didn't last long when Frankie drew on her Wereall bloodline and relieved the she-devil of every ounce of her powers. A side-effect of this had been Frankie ending up with more than a smidgeon of demon. It's something she's still coming to terms with, especially when it came to control. So far she's been lucky in that her inner demon has only shown itself when her anger gets the better of her.

"Could it be your grandpapa who 'as left the note?" Magda voices the thought that's been buzzing around in Frankie's brain like one of those flies down on the beach

Frankie adds Calico Jack to the list of suspects. She then adds Anne Bonny's name directly under his. Despite the woman being Frankie's grandmamma, she's under no illusions as to how lethal the ex-pirate can be. It's all there in black and white in the history books. Her grandparent's love of treasure being what it is, the warning could well be from them.

"What about the Wereall?" On the face of it, this is a good question from Dominik. But this is because he doesn't know the full effects of the spell Frankie put on the portal that leads to *All Hallows Keep*.

She's still coming to terms with the ancestry

that's made it possible for her to complete the spell. Not her fault some distant relation of hers got locked up for who knew what. Also not her fault the same relation managed to escape. That the witch was pregnant to one of the Wereall at the time is just the icing on the ancestry cake.

"It isn't possible for the Wereall to leave their realm right now." Frankie doesn't bother going into any further explanation.

Rather than maintain eye contact, Dominik stares off to the side. For a start, Frankie thinks he's decided he's better off playing hard to get. Then he speaks and blows this theory completely. "If the Wereall aren't able to leave, how do you explain that lot?"

As a unit everyone in the restaurant turns and looks in the same direction as the blond vampire. It's to see a troop of six Wereall in full battle fatigues marching toward the restaurant. There's nothing fluffy about these guys. If Frankie were to hazard a guess she'd say legs of a rhino, gorilla torso, arms of an orangutan and a head that's pure demon, complete with horns. Even with everything in proportion, the combo is ugly as sin.

3

Never has Frankie been more pleased to have gained full-ish control of her magical powers. She's also glad of all that extra training Zane forced on her. She immediately throws up a spell that will have anyone looking into the restaurant seeing what was there before. A room full of smashed furniture, settled dust and neglect. Better they see this than the current set-up being as it's like something you'd see in a high-end furniture showroom.

While she's doing this Zane magically locks all the doors and windows, physically barring entrance to the guards. This way, it'll only be the six burly Wereall guards not being able to get cold drinks that'll cause consternation.

Everything magical being taken care of, Sophie shuts down the air conditioning unit and the room descends into a deathly hush. Nana Peg, the vampires and the two familiars stay where they are. Having done everything they can, Zane, Frankie and Sophie settle once more into their seats. Actual relaxation doesn't come as easily.

Even knowing the guards can't get to them, it's hard to stay calm; especially when the first guard stiff-arms the doors, obviously expecting them to open. Instead, the doors remain closed and he smashes into the glass panels, with the doors rattling alarmingly. He gives the doors another almighty shove, but still they stay shut.

Him having failed, the others each take a turn before they throw their combined weight at the doors. Zane's spell stays solid, as do the doors.

The guards then try the windows. Again they stay intact. The largest pane of glass even holds out when a patio chair is thrown at it. The chair bouncing back and hammering the guard who threw has Frankie snickering in delight.

On spotting a couple of the guards disappearing around the corner of the building, Frankie turns to Zane. "I sure hope you locked ALL the doors and windows."

His only response is to raise an eyebrow. It's enough for her to sink back into the sofa. She should know the Nautilus is nothing if not thorough.

It's at least another quarter hour of mayhem before the guards leave, cussing and swearing. At least this is what Nana Peg says they're doing, with them speaking in a language none of the group is familiar with. Certainly it's nothing the Babel spell can translate for Frankie or Zane. Perhaps this is because the language of the Wereall isn't of this world?

Frankie taps her pen against the pad on her lap. "Okay, so I think we can safely add the Wereralls to the list of suspects." She's still not sure how it is the guards are on the island. That is unless there's a portal to the Wereall realm that she doesn't know about. To be honest, it wouldn't surprise her. If she was a guard in a place as hideous as *All Hallows Keep*, she'd sure want there to be more than one way in, or out.

Frankie turns to her Wereall relation. "Nana Peg, did they say why they're here?" Better to know if the guards have simply snuck out for a cold drink and not that they're actively guarding the place. Another option is that they weren't at the keep when Frankie put the suspension hex in place. This would have them stuck in the human realm in their Wereall form, just like her nana.

It's a moment before the Wereall replies, and then it's with a question. "Was William at the keep when you left?"

Frankie laughs in remembrance of the Wereall in his human form, locked in the large armoire in his bathroom. "Oh heck, yes he was."

"Hmmm. This means he's no longer at the keep."

Frankie straightens in her seat. "What! Why?"

"Because those aren't just any guards, they're imperial guards and where William goes, they go. So if they're here, then..."

There's no need for Nana Peg to continue.

"Blast, I thought I'd sealed the place up, nice and tight. If there's another portal, then how come you can't get back home?"

"I'm not sure, dear. It might be that only William can activate the portal he and his guards are using."

"In that case, why are they stuck in their animal form?"

Frankie thinks back on the guards at *All Hallows Keep* and their appearance of having been patched together. The imperial guards are anything but. To a Wereall, they're identical in their assembly. Still ugly but a heck of a lot tidier.

"They're not stuck like that. Imperial guards rarely take their human form. To them humans are weak. Certainly humans are weaker than a Wereall harnessing the power of their totem."

"So... definitely not here on holiday then?"

Nana Peg shakes her head at Dominik's suggestion.

Frankie looks down at the pad on her knee, crosses out Wereall and replaces it with a single name, William. From what she's seen of Wereall hierarchy, she doubts very much those guards are killing of their own volition.

Even though the list is short, and the space they have to search not large, it's not going to be a walk in the park. Before any sorties can take place, they need all the supplies from the *Pearl*. It's something Frankie undertakes without thinking. The restaurant goes from being reasonably empty to having all their goods stacked against the back wall.

However, the room isn't completely crammed, with a good amount of space left over for the team to limber up and practice their set moves. No point them having trained as hard as they have if they don't maintain this. Without powers in the realm of the Wereall, it will be their natural skills that will keep them safe. Well, apart from Frankie that is. There are pluses to having Wereall lineage. She won't need half of what's contained in the stacks of plastic boxes in the restaurant.

Most surprising is that amidst these modern containers is a large wooden crate. Frankie knows it belongs to the vampires, but she has no idea what's inside. Perhaps it contains spare teeth? Surely they're a vampire's main weapon?

Apart from Magda that is. All the woman needs to do is look at a guard and their energy levels plummet along with their bottom jaw. She, like all the vampires Frankie has seen, is gorgeous. It's this that stuns her enemy allowing her to take their energy without a hint of resistance.

Even women don't appear to be completely immune.

The dust kicked up by the arrival of their supplies hasn't settled before Sophie is ferreting through the largest plastic container. Most unusual about this is that it's a solid black, rather than translucent like all the others. The small witch had said light would affect her explosives, even making a 'boom' gesture to reinforce this.

Those explosives being stored aboard the *Pearl*, Frankie wasn't taking any chances. A black plastic container it was, and as solid a black as she could get it too.

The vampires soon follow Sophie's actions, levering the top off their crate with a tyre iron. As to where this came from, Frankie's in the dark. A minute later and she no longer has to wonder about the contents of the crate. The first thing Dominik pulls free is a wicked looking crossbow. He hands this to Luca before once again bending over the large crate. Mmmm, she should maybe have conjured up some baggier shorts for him.

Frankie spins away from the cute vampire. A quick look at Zane and she knows she hasn't broadcast her thoughts. Phew, that was close. Once again under control, she turns back to find Dominik handing out another crossbow. This time to Magda. All these weapons don't sit well with Frankie. Sure they're going up against a deadly foe, but should this mean they need to sink to that level too?

She's about to say something when she sees the size of the arrows. They're teeny. Only on closer inspection does she see the ends have been dipped in something. She walks over to take a closer look. "What's on the end of them?" She's about to touch one, when Dominik smacks her hand away with more force than Frankie feels is necessary. "Owww, careful." She rubs her wrist, checking for damage.

Dominik is immediately contrite and Frankie doubts it's got anything to do with Zane storming across the room. "I'm sorry I hurt you. If you'd touched the tip, you'd have been out cold for at least twelve hours."

"So, not lethal then?"

Dominik hesitates before answering. It's long enough to have Frankie wondering if there are different types of arrows in the crate. She's about to press the vampire on it when Zane takes her hand gently in his. Frankie's not having a bar of it. "It's nothing. Come on, we need to get ready to check the place out." She's also conscious of hiding any bruising that might develop.

They're finally ready to set out to explore the rest of the resort when they spot the imperial guard in the distance. They're carrying what looks to be a coconut palm trunk, no doubt intending to use it as a make-shift battering ram.

Frankie screws up her nose and grabs her wand from a pocket on her cargo shorts. She's then at a loss, not having a clue as to the right sort of spell to deal with this. "Now what do we do?"

Zane, who's also holding his wand up, doesn't look as nonplussed. "The doors will hold, but it might be better to get rid of them altogether."

"But... but... if you say they'll hold, why'd we want to get rid of them?"

Zane snorts and chokes back laughter before replying. "Not the doors, the guards."

Frankie stares open-mouthed at him. Sure he's up for cracking a few heads together, but she's never heard him talk of straight-out murder. She thought that was Dominik's department.

Zane looks at her, his brow knotted before comprehension arrives. "I don't mean kill them, just send them somewhere. Where would you like to dispatch them to, Shortcake?"

Frankie's still confused as to what he's getting at. "What do you mean?"

"With the correct incantation we can turn the restaurant doors into a mini portal of sorts."

"So we can send them to hell?" Frankie crosses her fingers, hoping this is an option.

Zane laughs, before responding. "Unfortunately, no. But we can send them to anywhere on the island."

At last Frankie understands what he's getting

at. "The end of the dock would be funny. A nice dip will cool them off better than a cold drink."

Zane grins broadly and is joined by the rest of the group. Even Dex is baring his teeth while snickering telepathically.

"Shortcake, if you stand on that side of the door, I'll take this side. Sophie, I'll get you to stand in front of the doors."

Frankie's soon in position and ready to act, even if she still has no idea what she's meant to be doing. She gains some degree of confidence on looking at Zane and Sophie, who are also in position. On seeing them pointing their wands at the middle of the doors, Frankie follows suit.

"Okay, repeat after me." Zane waits to get a nod from Frankie and Sophie before he continues.

> *These doors to a portal*
> *from here to the sea*
> *Bend space and time*
> *and help them fly free.*
> *In the blink of an eye*
> *and the beat of a heart*
> *Swift, true and straight*
> *we'll see them depart.*

Frankie's pleased Zane says the incantation as slowly as he does, allowing her and Sophie to follow along a word or two behind him. This results in sparks flying out the end of the three wands, with these coalescing in a tight ball by the door handles. No sooner do they finish the spell than the sparks spread out coating the doors in a blinding shimmer.

A second later the end of the coconut palm trunk hits the doors smack bang in the middle, and Sophie throws herself to one side. Rather than there being a huge crash, the guards go through the doors although they don't actually enter the restaurant itself. It's more like they disappear into the doors themselves.

Frankie rushes over to the windows that face the beach. She doesn't have to wait long with the six guards and their trunk soon appearing at the end of the dock. Momentum then carries them and the make-shift battering ram off the end. After hovering for a second, they drop from sight. There follows a thoroughly satisfying splash.

A wave of Zane's wand and the double doors swing inward, allowing the group to leave. They're all out in the courtyard when Zane turns back toward the restaurant doors. He reseals them, barring entrance to the Wereall. "Okay, while they take a dip, let's spread out. Keep your eyes peeled for anything and anybody."

"Am I going with you, Mom?"

"Of course you are. We're a team." Frankie also doesn't trust her familiar not to get himself into a whole heap of trouble if he's on his own.

"Remember we've practiced our set moves together."

Thankfully he takes her at her word, with there being no need to talk him out of trotting off on his own. Likewise Sophie's familiar, Stinky the hamster, is going to be searching with her witch.

What Frankie isn't expecting is Dominik, with a crossbow slung over one shoulder, waiting to accompany her and the Jack Russell. She knows this has nothing to do with her being able to take care of herself. She lifts an eyebrow in a maneuver designed to have him backing off. It doesn't work, so she spells it out for the gorgeous vampire. "It'll be better if you strike out on your own. We can cover more ground that way. Also, I don't actually need your help."

Dex snakes around her ankles until he's between her and the vampire. *"You don't need him when I'm around."*

"You got that right, buddy." Frankie doesn't go into any more detail than this with the majority of time it being her looking after Dex and not the other way around.

Dominik grins broadly before replying to her. "I was hoping you could protect me."

Frankie snorts, so ludicrous is this scenario. She's not being taken in for a second. "Off you go." Not waiting for him to leave her to it, she waves her wand transporting him to the other side of the resort. He's as far from her destination as possible and with luck won't have merged with anyone on arrival.

"Nice work, Shortcake. You saved me having to do it myself." A brief kiss to her lips and Zane does an about turn and heads toward the opposite side of the resort.

Luca and Magda set out together; their destination the jungle villa Frankie and the others had stayed in before. If Anne and Calico Jack are staying on the island, then this is surely where they'll make their headquarters. Apart from the deck giving a good view of the resort, it's the best accommodation on offer.

Sophie opts to search the beach and the front of the resort. Stinky, who's stuffed down the front of the witch's blouse, swivels her head in tandem with her witch. It's cute enough that Frankie's unable to stop herself from breaking into a broad smile.

"Right Dex, let's go see if we can't spot some baddies." From here on, she's going to communicate with him telepathically. This way, even if things get noisy, he'll still be able to hear her clearly, and vice versa. It's also how they've practiced.

Frankie knows exactly where she and Dex are heading. If the welcome note and package has been courtesy of her grandparents, she's got a good idea where they'll be digging.

She and Dex travel cross-country to the tennis courts, avoiding the paths. No point sneaking around if you're going to advertise your location when the crushed shells on the paths move. There's also less chance of bumping into anyone this way, although it would be the Goddess's own bad luck if they did.

No sooner has this thought crossed her mind than her senses pick up on something. *"Stop, Dex, by my side!"* Frankie clicks her fingers urgently. Only when he's hard up against her leg does she remember the concealment spell. Perhaps it's because she doesn't feel any different that it's hard to remember in the heat of the moment?

Normally, all they'd have to do would be to stand still or move quietly out the way of the other person or persons. Trouble is when they're invisible too, that's not exactly easy.

If not for Frankie detecting the raw energy, she wouldn't have had a clue someone was even there.

But there they are.

And, if her senses are correct, they're getting closer.

4

Frankie does her best to slow her breathing. She even throws an extra veil of silence over herself and Dex as insurance. If Zane's spell were to fail, it would be a first. Is this going to stop her from backing it up with something extra of her own? Bejinxed barnacles no it isn't.

Once again she concentrates on the energy being emitted from whoever it is closing in on them. The only person on the island who should be able to cloak themselves like this is Calico Jack and, by extension, Anne. And Frankie isn't ready to deal with them just yet.

Dex sniffs the air. It sounds loud to her, and she has to fight the need to tell him to be quiet. There's no way whoever it is should be able to hear her or the Jack Russell.

"Can you pick anything up?" The only way the dog won't be able to, is if the new arrival is using a

cover-up spell as bullet-proof as Zane's. And backed up with something similar to hers.

"Coconut oil. With high notes of steak. Hmmm, mushrooms on the side."

Thank the Goddess the new arrivals are simply invisible and not masked completely. The dog picking up on these scents firmly identifies the new arrivals as Anne and Jack. The steak and mushrooms won't have been cooked in coconut oil. It's that her grandmamma smothers herself in the stuff when she's sunbathing. And for a redhead to do this tells Frankie that Calico Jack has come up with an SPF250 spell of his own.

Frankie looks at the ground, deep in thought as to what she should do. The moment they found the guards on the beach, all their carefully made plans had gone out the porthole. Should she confront her relatives, or keep quiet? She's still dwelling on it when she hears Zane inside her head.

"You've found something. I can hear the cogs in your brain whirring from here."

Rather than deny he's correct, Frankie responds. *"I've found Calico Jack and Anne, but they don't know I'm here."*

"What are they wearing?"

So bizarre is this question, Frankie doesn't bother telling him she can't see them. *"Why on earth would you want to know that?"*

"Because if they're in resort wear, they're hardly going to be on a killing spree, are they?"

He's got a point. Shame she doesn't have a clue what they've got on. It's something she tells him

"Okay, leave them be for now. We knew they'd be here because of the boat. See who else you can track down. I'm keen to know if William is on the island as Peggy says."

It's a strategy Frankie's agrees with. Rather than risk discovery by Calico Jack courtesy of his magical powers, Frankie transports herself and Dex to their original destination. No point risking detection this early in the piece. It also means she's free to examine the tennis courts in the knowledge her relatives are a good way away, at least for now that is.

On arrival Frankie and Dex look through the wire fence that surrounds the courts. On the face of it these look to be as damaged as they had been last time they were here. It's then that Frankie spots a shovel. This is definitely new. Any earlier damage had been the result of Sophie lobbing explosives over the net like she was at Flushing Meadows.

"Let's check out what they've been up to."

Frankie and Dex walk around the tennis courts, looking into each and every crater they come across. The biggest is still that which had seen the odious Captain Russell Garnet blown to smithereens. It's something that has Frankie rubbing her finger where the cut that wouldn't heal had been. This has her smiling at thoughts of Gwen Morris subsisting on cockroaches thanks to her part in the blood hex. It serves the evil witch right.

There's nothing in any of the holes to suggest Calico Jack and Anne have stumbled across any new booty. Here's hoping their continued digging will keep them out of Frankie and the other's way. The last thing they need is a couple of stragglers following them through the cliff leading to *All Hallows Keep*.

She's about to head to their next location, when she stills. It wouldn't be fair to make it too easy for her grandparents to dig up more treasure, would it? Frankie executes an all-encompassing wave of her wand over the courts, even spinning in place to do so. There isn't a piece of the grass courts left untainted by her spell. Perfect, their digging will be just a little harder from here on in. About time those two worked for their money.

"Right let's go see if we can find some bad guys."

Dex, trotting in her wake, Frankie starts a zigzag pattern, searching any building in their path. She also keeps an eye out for more Wereall guards and any evidence that they've been around. Strangely she doesn't find anything. She doesn't even run into any of the resort's security guards, dead or alive. They'd been in abundant supply on her earlier visits to the resort.

It had been one of them who nearly killed Dex by blasting the poor dog with a Taser. It's something that still has Frankie's breathing ramping up. She never wants to hold his lifeless body in her arms again. Like ever.

The pair is close to being back at the restaurant when Frankie spots something that has her anger spiking. It's Zane, and he's lying next to one of the resort's swimming pools. The cocktail on the small table by his sun lounger is sporting more umbrellas than a lost property department.

That he's fast asleep is the last straw for Frankie. It is not okay for him to be snoring away while the rest of the team combs the resort for clues.

"What the heck? We've all been stomping around in this heat and here you are sunning yourself and drinking cocktails. Are you for real?" Frankie knows there's a hard edge to her telepathic voice, but really?

"Sunning myself? What do you mean? I'm in the jungle to the east of the resort. More mosquitos than mojitos over this way."

"Then who..." Frankie answers her own question. She knows exactly who it is. This says more clearly than an engraved invitation that he knows she's on the island. *"I've just found the Wereall's commander, William."*

"Where are you?"

Frankie squints at the nearest signpost. No point saying she's by the pool when the resort boasts three of them. Better if she can name the exact one.

"I'm by the Bali Bali Pool." Hmmph, so good they named it twice, although they could at least have picked a local name.

A moment later Zane is standing next to her and Dex. His expression on seeing who's lying beside the pool, is as incredulous as her own has been. This then morphs into a broad grin.

"I don't see what's so great about him masquerading as you."

"Don't you? Remember he takes on the form that is guaranteed to be most pleasing to his target."

Zane's right. And even if it says William knows she's on the island, there's no need for the merman to get ahead of himself.

Frankie concentrates as hard as she can on Dominik and is delighted to see the man lying next to the pool is now a spitting image of the hunky vampire. There having been no reaction from William, Frankie realizes he isn't able to tell he's changed shape courtesy of her concentration. It might be a different story if he was awake.

Taking pity on Zane, Frankie then concentrates as hard as she can on her canine sidekick. Even Zane bursts out laughing on seeing that there's a Jack Russell lying on the sun lounger.

"Okay, enough mucking about. Put him back how he was."

There's whining from ankle height to this suggestion. *"Awww, can't we leave him like that, he looks so handsome!"*

Despite Dex's gripes, Frankie again thinks of Zane and William is back to resembling the merman. She then takes a moment to admire how gorgeous Zane looks in swimming trunks. It's not the first time she's seen his chest. It is however the first time she's seen him oiled up like that.

Zane crosses his arms and raises an eyebrow. "You finished ogling me yet."

"Sorry, you're so pretty." Frankie gives him a practiced smile before continuing. "Let's get back to the restaurant and see if the others have spotted anyone." Other than the imperial guard, they could have seen members of the security team, or even the Garnet family.

They don't risk transporting themselves there; they walk side-by-side, with Dex bringing up the rear. For all they know, the courtyard out front of the restaurant could be teeming with Wereall guards. It makes more sense to approach slowly avoiding the potential for merging with one of the hairy beasts.

Sure enough, when they round the corner of a nearby building, they can see the imperial guard is there. They're hanging around right in front of the double doors leading to the restaurant. Even though Zane and Frankie can get themselves and Dex inside the building without the guards being aware, it's painful to have them stationed right where they are. It's unsettling more than anything, like having a Peeping Tom outside your lounge 24/7.

"To heck with this." Frankie pulls her wand from its pocket. She then waves it in the direction of the Bali Bali Pool. Even as far away as they are, they're still able to hear William's reaction. There was no way he was going to sleep through having half the contents of the pool dumped on him. A moment later the imperial guard storms by. "That should keep them out of our hair for a while."

Their way clear, they wander over to the restaurant. Because of the type of ward Zane had placed earlier, there's no need to use a wand to enter. He simply touches the doors and they open wide allowing them to enter the air-conditioned comfort of the large room.

They're the last to return with all the others stretched out, drinking sodas and generally taking it easy. Dominik's expression when he looks at Frankie is thoughtful. The smile that follows says he's not giving up as easily as she'd like.

It's something that has her heart beating faster. She can't work out if this is because she's happy about his continued pursuit, or not. It'll be something that will have the imperial guards scratching their hairy heads.

She imagines William's appearance is currently swapping back and forth between Dominik and Zane. She's glad the Nautilus isn't able to witness this.

Hoping to really freak them out, Frankie looks at Dex. She even scratches his side to strengthen the connection. If she's right, one of William's legs will be twitching uncontrollably right about now. Oh, she could have some fun with this. And it serves William right if he's going to dig around in her subconscious without her permission.

There's not even been time for a round up from the group when Frankie nearly drops her can of soda. It's the double doors swinging open of their own accord that's given her a fright. They shouldn't be able to do that, should they?

Even unable to see anyone, Frankie, like Sophie and Zane is pointing her wand toward the open space at the entrance. The air starts to sparkle, and then Anne and Calico Jack pop into focus. Anne's wearing a dark green bikini and armed with what looks to be an antique firearm.

The pair scans the restaurant, with their lack of reaction proving the camouflage ward is still up and running. Frankie keeps a wary eye on her grandparents as they wander aimlessly around the space. She finds it fascinating that neither of them bangs into the furniture. They'll be walking directly at a sofa or chair and then swerve at the last moment. "Do we reveal ourselves to them, or not?"

Zane appears to think about it, but only for a second. "I don't think there's any point in hiding from them. They obviously know someone's here." He's waves his wand, resulting in exclamations of surprise from both Calico Jack and Anne. They quickly regroup by the front doors.

No sooner are they together than Anne points her blunderbuss straight at Frankie's chest. It's hardly the usual greeting from a grandparent.

Frankie doesn't even bother using her wand; instead she waves her hand negligently in her grandmamma's direction. This sees the firearm shrinking rapidly in size until it is so small it slips through Anne's fingers. How dare her grandmamma threaten her like this?

Aware Zane and Dominik are both staring at her Anne's teeny bikini, Frankie waves her hand again. Okay, so pink thermals aren't exactly ideal clothing for the tropics, but Frankie doesn't care. She wasn't keen on the way Zane's pupils were dilating like that.

Anne crosses her arms, her annoyance easy to see. Frankie thinks it's down to the hideous outfit she's lumbered Anne with until her grandmamma speaks. "You will not have it!"

It wouldn't take a brain surgeon to work out what it is the woman's talking about. "Hard as it will be for you to believe, not all of us share your avarice." This isn't to say Frankie would say no to a share of the treasure. Technically it's her inheritance, and her bank balance is getting alarmingly low. While she can magic up food for herself and Dex, paying for the utilities at the marina is starting to prove problematic.

Calico Jack tilts his head to one side, unable to believe Frankie isn't after their treasure. "Then what are you here for?"

Does Frankie tell him, or not? Zane is screaming in her head to keep their mission quiet for now. "*Make something up! Anything!*"

"*Anything?*"

His last instruction right as Frankie speaks is, "*Make it believable.*"

5

Zane's warning comes too late, far too late. Frankie's already blurting out the first thing that's popped into her head.

"We're on holiday."

Now it's Calico Jack's turn to fold his arms and glare at her. "On holiday?"

"Yep. Ah, we were, ah, all so exhausted after giving Zane his energy back, that we ah... We needed a break."

Calico Jack grins, and for a moment Frankie thinks he's believed her. "And that lot?"

Sure he's referring to the vampires, Frankie glances in their direction. She's relieved to see there are no crossbows on show. It's then she grasps Calico Jack's looking at the group's supplies and not the vampires. He's not alone in staring in disbelief. Zane is doing a fair amount of this himself. Unfortunately, he's looking at her.

"This is the best you could come up with, Shortcake?"

Frankie attempts to dig herself out of the hole of her own making. "It's an extended break. We weren't sure what would be available on the island."

"And *Boom-Boom*? What's she doing here?"

It doesn't take a rocket scientist to know Calico Jack is referring to Sophie, the coven's explosives expert. Frankie hasn't come up with a reason for the witch's presence when Sophie answers him herself.

"I'm here in my role as coven healer. Zane's still convalescing."

This time rather than smiling, Calico Jack bursts into peals of laughter. Strange then that he doesn't sound amused. "The only thing you're good at is blowing stuff up. And you're hopeless at that too."

Sophie's annoyance is obvious, with the small witch shaking due to her efforts to stop herself from retaliating. She's no match for someone of Calico Jack's capabilities and she knows it. Taking him on would see her in a world of pain if not dead.

Frankie's having none of it. The victim of bullies when she was younger, she's not letting her granddad get away with it. His attention on Sophie, Calico Jack doesn't see Frankie twitch her wand. Okay so she's kinda sneaky about it too. She is after all his granddaughter.

Calico Jack goes to fire more abuse at Sophie, but nothing comes out. It's enough to for him to know he's been jinxed. His gaze darts around the room before landing on Frankie. Without breaking eye contact, he points at his voice box and a small spark shoots out the end of his finger. This hits his throat just above his Adam's apple and is immediately absorbed.

He opens his mouth again and Frankie waits for him to speak. Nothing comes out, abuse or otherwise. Perfect.

Now it's her grandmamma who's glaring at Frankie. "What have you done to my Jacky?"

"Oh, relax would you? He'll be fine once he leaves here."

"Zap her Jacky. Zap her good." Without a musket in her hand, Anne is aware she's no match for her granddaughter. If she attacks Frankie, she knows she'll end up on the ground in a heap soon after. It's this that has her spurring Frankie's granddad on to take her out magically. In most families this would be a no-no, but these members of the clan are as dysfunctional as they come.

Calico Jack dutifully points a finger at Frankie and mouths an incantation. It's something that has Zane throwing a ward up in front of her. She didn't need it, but it's still nice to have. As a symbol of his affection, it's way more useful than half-a-dozen red roses.

"Do you really think I'm that stupid, granddad?" Frankie's use of this moniker has him fuming, as it always does. It's why she's used it. It's about time he knows what it's like to feel weak. "Your magic doesn't work in here."

Zane swivels, and stares at her. "Did you just execute a double?"

"Actually, it was a triple." Frankie tries not to sound overly proud of this accomplishment.

"A triple!"

Sophie's exclamation is high-pitched enough that Dex swipes at his ears with his front paws.

Zane looks carefully at Calico Jack before turning back to Frankie. "What was the third spell?"

Rather than 'spell' it out, Frankie demonstrates to everyone what the final part of her jinx has been.

She looks at Anne until their eyes lock and then keeps eye contact until her grandmamma's eyes widen. "Grandmamma, tell us everything you know about the two guards on the beach."

Only once Anne and Calico Jack have left the restaurant and are no longer visible, does Zane speak. "Well, that was interesting." He then reinstates their camo spell. It's something Frankie is pleased about, too easy to forget when it is, and isn't, in place.

"I always knew she was cold blooded, but that? That takes the biscuit." Frankie shudders as she goes back over what her grandmamma said. "To walk right by them and do nothing is incomprehensible." It would have been one thing if the guards were already dead. But no, according to Anne they'd even pleaded with her to free them or at least bring them water. "Nothing to do with me," had been her flippant response to Frankie's outrage at her doing nothing.

Frankie finds it hard to believe she's related to someone this callous. Sure Anne was dealt a bad hand early in life, but bad enough to wipe any human kindness from her soul? Would Frankie have it in her to do something like this? She's still mulling this over when she notices movement nearby.

Dominik is next to the restaurant's doors, ready to open them. In response to her look of query, he simply says, "Be back in a moment."

So rapid is his departure that the doors are left swinging. All Frankie sees as he crosses the courtyard is a blur. The vamp sure can move. As to where he's gone, Frankie appears to be as in the dark as Zane and Sophie.

The only two in the room who don't seem mystified by his actions are Magda and Luca.

Magda snuggles in closer to Luca and only when comfortable, does she speak. "I do not think they believe you with your story of our 'oliday." She then shrugs as if this is neither here nor there.

Luca, who's been nodding in agreement with this wife, adds his own thoughts on Frankie's lie. "It was maybe not the best."

Frankie holds her hands up to stop any further recriminations in their tracks. She knows she's messed up, without those two pointing it out. Lying doesn't come naturally to her, especially not when she's put on the spot like that. She hasn't said anything in her defense when Dominik returns.

He throws himself back into his seat, his face split in a broad grin. "That's sorted them out."

Frankie leans forward in anticipation. When he doesn't say anything, she spits out, "Okay, give. Who?"

"Hah, your grandparents. They have no idea."

Frankie tilts her head to the side in a fair imitation of Dex. Nope, it doesn't do any good she still doesn't have a clue what he's on about. "No idea of what?"

"That we're not here on holiday. That we're all convalescing as we re-build our energy stores. There are pigs on the island, aren't there?"

Frankie nods dumbly in answer to this seemingly random question.

Zane twists around in his seat, so he too is

looking at the blond vampire. "You tweaked their memories, didn't you?"

Rather than speak, Dominik nods slowly. He's the personification of smug.

Frankie stares at him, mouth agape. "I thought that was an old wives' tale?"

He shakes his head, also slowly. His bearing is still high on the smug scale.

Frankie's read about this, in freaking novels. That it's true is hard to comprehend, even if it's amazing, and incredibly helpful. At least they don't need to worry about having to convince Anne and Calico Jack why they're on the island.

Frankie retrieves her pad and pen from the coffee table. She crosses Anne's name off the list of suspects. She doesn't however cross off that of Calico Jack. Just because Anne didn't actively take part in pegging the two guards out on the sand, this isn't to say her granddad didn't. He could have had the guards staked out with a single wave of his wand and Anne would be none the wiser.

Frankie knows crossing her grandmamma's name off is a technicality. By not helping the guards when they were alive, she's as responsible for their deaths as whoever did the deed.

"Okay, so what did everyone see while they were out and about?" Frankie points her pen at Luca and Magda. "Do you want to go first?" She's honestly not expecting them to report a lot, with the pair only having eyes for each other. She hopes to heck the googly eyes stop when they're at *All Hallows Keep*.

It's Magda who answers for the pair. "We visit jungle villa. This is where your grandparents they stay." On seeing Frankie's reaction to this assertion, Magda presses on. "Many bikinis, so many bikinis." It's proof enough for Frankie.

When she falls silent, Luca continues. "And there was more steak in the fridge than I've seen at some abattoirs."

It takes all Frankie's willpower not to grill Luca on his knowledge of abattoirs. Even so, she's got an idea as to why.

"Hmmm, steak! What did I tell you?" pipes up Dex, who's been strangely, quiet since their return to the restaurant.

"Did you see anyone who might belong to the Garnet family?"

As one, Luca and Magda shake their heads.

Next Frankie points her pen at Dominik. "What about you? Did you spot anyone?"

"I did." The vampire then falls silent, his brow wrinkled in thought.

"And?" Frankie's unable to keep the edge out of her voice with this single word. The last thing she needs is attitude from him because she's rebuking his advances. Not helpful. Not helpful at all. If he's going to keep this up, he can go home. And she doesn't care how handy he'll be when they breach the keep.

"I did see someone, at first..." He waves his hands in the air before continuing. "She looked like you. And yet I knew it wasn't you."

"And why is that?"

"When I approached her, she flirted with me." Dominik's chagrin at this has Zane smiling in delight.

Nana Peg, who's been rustling up sandwiches from their supplies, puts a plate down in front of Frankie. "It'll be one of the Wereall. Only we can replicate another like that."

Frankie grabs a sandwich from the teetering pile and takes a bite, chewing thoughtfully. She's about to take another bite when she stops herself. "So you're saying there's another Wereall female on the island?" Her question out there, she attacks her sandwich again.

Nana Peg pats Frankie's shoulder. "No dear, it'll be one of the imperial guards."

Frankie nearly chokes. Her first reaction is to be peeved that one of those hairy beasts is pretending to be her. Then she thinks on why that would be. It makes no sense. "If it was one of the guards, how come they didn't take Dominik out?"

"Ah, yeah." Dominik dry washes his face before continuing. "As soon as I realized it wasn't you, I latched onto their mind. They didn't know what hit them." It was his controlling their thoughts that had them turning around and walking away, leaving him in peace. "I made sure they won't even remember meeting me."

Zane, who's been quiet throughout the exchange, coughs to break the tension. "You know, the Wereall aren't alone in being able to masquerade as others."

Frankie wrinkles her brow in concentration and is soon rewarded with an image. It's one that has her shivering in recollection. She knows of one other entity capable of that sort of transformation. The Succubus, Mimi Merriweather. "But she's dead." Frankie knows this because she's the one responsible for the demise of the she-devil.

Zane initially shrugs in response before speaking. "It's something to think on."

Frankie thinks on it and even adds a couple of question marks to the list of potential killers.

Nana Peg and Sophie having reported their findings, it becomes apparent there's no one from the Garnet family on the island, at least none wandering around freely. Frankie has to fight the urge to race to the top of the island, plant a flag and claim it back for the Bonny family. It might be that the Garnets are simply in hiding somewhere on the island. Somewhere the team has missed. A large percentage of the island is made up of jungle and it's therefore impossible for them to search it all. Unless…

"Magda, you know how you can sense energy."

"Yes, this is so."

"Can I do that too?"

Rather than respond in words, Magda simply shrugs. Luca joins his wife with a similar gesture. Even Dominik is looking unsure of himself, for once.

Frankie jumps to her feet. "I'll be back soon. Dex, you stay here." The small dog who's nibbling the remains of her sandwich, doesn't argue. A wave of her wand and Frankie once again finds herself atop the tallest spot on the island, affording her 360-degree views. All she's missing is a flag.

Not sure what she's doing, she's happy there's no-one here to witness her potential failure. Despite having been in possession of her vampire senses for a week or two, she's done nothing with them. At least not on purpose.

This is about to change.

Frankie shoves her wand into a pocket of her cargo shorts and then holds her arms wide. Her eyes shut, she allows her senses to heighten, imagining them spanning out over the island. The first thing she becomes aware of is a family of pigs nearby. Mom, dad and half a dozen little ones, if she's not mistaken.

She's flooded with energy before she knows what's happening. She shuts it down as soon as she can, although not fast enough. Ooops, daddy pig is out cold and mummy is a little shaky on her feet. Another check and she's relieved to find the small porkers are as perky in their play as previously. *Wow, there's a tongue twister.*

"Concentrate, Shortcake."

Following a nudge from Zane, Frankie once again expands her senses. This time she's careful not to siphon anyone or anything's energy in the process. First she searches the back of the island and isn't surprised when she only comes across wildlife. She then turns to her right and repeats the process.

That's odd. Even if the Garnets have left in their droves, shouldn't she be able to pick up the imperial guard, and William? As it is all she can detect is parrots, pigs and assorted reptiles.

It's a different story when she turns and faces left.

Frankie immediately picks up on someone. Not a Wereall, but a regular guy. She doesn't know why she's sure of this, but she is. She's also surprised to find she can sense how old he is and that he's super tall. As to his appearance, that's a big old blank.

It's where he's standing that causes her the most consternation. While not able to see him, she is able to see through his eyes. She'd recognize that cliff face anywhere. The runes carved into the rock confirm it one hundred percent. She knows because she carved them.

She can do nothing as she watches him hold

his hand out and point an amulet similar to hers at the runes. Rather than the amulet lighting up as Frankie expects, the rock face explodes, showering him with rubble.

The noise of the explosion reaches her atop the hill, confirming she hasn't imagined it. She does her best to reconnect to the guy in hopes of seeing what's become of the cliff face.

She connects alright.

Unfortunately, there's nothing to see, unless you count a solid, unforgiving black that's in danger of sucking her in hook, line and soul.

6

Frankie struggles to free herself from the dead man's mind. It's not easy, and she's close to freaking out before she escapes. She gives herself a second to deal with the heebie jeebies before waving her wand. This has her standing next to a ten-foot pile of rocks. Of the person responsible for the rock fall there's not a lot to see. That is apart from a hand poking out the top of the mini mountain.

A quick search with her senses confirms he's dead. It's something she kinda knew already, but it pays to check these things. She's also been careful not to merge her energies with his. She is NEVER doing that again.

It's definitely not Calico Jack. The residual magic filling the clearing isn't his nor is it from the guy who's borne the brunt of the rock slide. The dead man is human through-and-through.

He could be a member of the Garnet family.

Frankie can't help but wonder if he's the one responsible for the death of her mom. If he is, then he deserves everything he's got.

Even though the magic in the clearing isn't Calico Jack's, it is familiar. As to why that is, Frankie can't say. She's felt it before, although perhaps not in its present form.

The one thing she's sure of is that the guy is no longer holding the amulet, nor is it on the ground nearby. She's about to start moving rocks when Zane pops into focus next to her. Dex is with him.

"See Dex, I told you she was okay." Zane ensures he's got Frankie's attention before he continues. "I could sense it." It appears enough of a revelation to him that he's got both eyebrows raised.

Obviously he's still coming to grips with the changes the energy meld that healed him have brought about. Frankie knows exactly how he feels, but tenfold. She's unable to suppress a shudder.

Frankie hunkers down and gives Dex a reassuring hug. "You were worried about me, buddy?"

"We heard a big bang. Sophie said it sounded magical."

Only after his trembling is under control does Frankie stand again. "Is that true?" Zane's blank look reminds her he can't hear her familiar. "Is it true that Sophie said it sounded magical?"

"That she did. She also said that whatever it was, it was big."

"*Boom-Boom* wasn't kidding. That's one hulking pile of rock."

Frankie spins to find Dominik right behind her. While his words might be light-hearted, his worried checking of every inch of her for damage is not.

Awww, he really does care for her. The grinding of teeth from her other side confirms she hasn't kept this thought from Zane. Ooops. *Tinfoil beanie, tinfoil beanie, tinfoil beanie.*

There's no way she's getting stuck in the middle of this particular alpha face-off. Better to hose it down pronto. Frankie does so by telling them what she'd seen through the dead man's eyes.

Leaving them to digest this new information, she leans down to give Dex another pat. Only he's no longer at her feet. No, he's scaling the rock pile as though it's Everest. Only when the pup has safely reached the top and sniffed the hand, does Frankie speak to him. "Is it anyone we know?"

Even though it's not Calico Jack, this isn't to say they haven't met the victim before. However brief it may have been, Dex will remember. With access to a Wereall amulet, this pegs the guy as either one of the Garnets, or even a relative of hers. Not that the amulet he was holding would be the same as her own. At least she doesn't think so, with all those she's seen so far having different backs.

The one thing she's still in the dark about is what the different runes are for. For Frankie they give her the ability to gain access to the We-reall realm. It had allowed Anne to rejoin the land of the living after near on one hundred years as a ghost. As to Calico Jack, who knew? He's always been super cagey about what his amulet is for. And Frankie doubts they're all one-hit-wonders. If they are, she's stuck with the magical equivalent of a glorified garage door opener.

"Come on, Dex. Stop mucking about. What can you smell?"

He looks down at her. She'd recognise that goofy expression any time. Surely not?

"Cake." It's all Dex can get out, so busy is he licking his chops.

"Dex!" Frankie's voice is loud in the relative quiet of the jungle. It's enough to get the small pup's attention. Only when he's looking at her, and not the hand, does she continue. "If you lick that hand, I'm gonna wash your mouth out with soap! You got that!"

His doggie disappointment is a palpable thing. Nevertheless he inches his way back down the rocks until he's once again at her feet.

"Why can't you hanker after dog food like a normal pooch? And what did you mean by cake?"

"That's what I could smell. High sugar content, chocolate frosting."

Sheesh, if his nose was any more finely tuned, he'd be able to rattle off the recipe and hints on decoration.

Dex safely next to her and the two males no longer eyeing each other up, Frankie starts removing rocks from the pile. She tosses these to the side, one-by-one. As tempting as it is to remove the rocks by magic, she worries the amulet might disappear along with them.

She's moved less than a dozen when she feels a hand on her shoulder. She knows it's not Zane for two reasons. The energy seeping into her back isn't his. And the grinding of his teeth says he's a couple of feet away from her. If he keeps reacting to Dominik like this, he's going to need dentures.

Dominik speaks, but not before taking his hand away rather hastily. "There is an easier way. Use your senses."

Frankie straightens, and moves to the side. This puts yet more distance between her and the uber cute vamp. "I can do that? I thought I could only sense living things."

"The energy of he who held the amulet will cling to it. But, you need to hurry before it fades."

This time when Frankie closes her eyes and puts her senses out, she feels silly. Fine when you're on your own atop a big hill, very different when you're standing between two gorgeous men. Hah, she's the filling in a hunk sandwich? She fights off the giggles, just, and goes back to searching for the amulet using her newly acquired vampire skills.

First she locks on to the residual energy of the person under the rocks. Then she spreads her senses out over the pile itself. Nope, the amulet isn't hidden amidst the rubble. She searches wider, taking in the whole resort. Nothing, she's not getting anything. She's about to open her eyes and search the old-fashioned way, when Dominik barks at her to try harder.

She squeezes her eyes tight shut and even holds her arms out to the side. She stretches her senses to the limit. Only then does she pick something up. It's faint and getting fainter.

She then goes all pointer-dog on them, spinning around and facing the resort. "This way!" She doesn't wait to see if they're following. She takes off all while keeping a lock on the faint magical signature she's picked up. This isn't easy to do while running, but she finds the closer she gets to it, the easier it becomes.

She's half way across the resort when Dex pulls up next to her.

"It's aaaages since we've been jogging together."

Rather than waste breath explaining that

they're not on a casual run, they're chasing someone, she simply grins down at him.

"Palm tree!"

She's wondering what on earth he's on about when she looks up and comes close to slamming into one. Only a quick step to the side, allows her to avoid a world of pain. Wow, she's never moved that fast before. Could this be something else she's picked up in the energy meld?

Or could it be something to do with her siphoning the powers of Natalia the self-appointed vampire queen?

It's something to add to her list of things to try later.

The energy being given off by the amulet is a palpable thing. For Frankie it's as though she could reach out and touch it. Shame it's not visible. She comes to another building, but rather than shoot around it and continue searching, her gut tells her to stop. It hasn't twanged like this in a while.

Listening to its tune, she pulls up next to the building and clicks her fingers to get Dex by her side. Zane and Dominik arrive a moment later, with neither man close to being out of breath. They really are a lot alike apart from their obvious differences. Frankie has to bite her lip to stop herself from smiling.

Dominik leans in and whispers in her ear. "I've searched here. There's nothing." Zane isn't having it. The Nautilus puts his large hard on Dominik's forehead and forcibly moves the vampire back.

"Ease up. He can't speak to me telepathically like you can. He was saying this is where he searched earlier. He said there was nothing here."

"And yet, here we are." Zane raises an eyebrow, and it's all Frankie can do not to lick her finger and smooch it back into place.

He does have a point, however.

"Hmmm, cake. Lots of sugar. Cream filling. Mmmm, chocolate frosting."

Wow, Dex really can sniff anything out. *"What brand of flour?"*

"Not sure, but it's plenty light and fluffy."

Light and fluffy? Frankie looks down to find Dex jamming his face into a large slice of cake on a paper plate. She hadn't seen that when they first rocked up. Are her powers of observation slipping?

"Where did you find that?"

He yawns widely before he can answer. *"It was just lying here. Honest."* He yawns again. *"Oooh, I'm so sleepy."* He keels over a second later.

In the past this would have had Frankie in a panic. Fortunately she's able to sense his energy levels are still strong. Sure he's been drugged, but thankfully, it isn't life-threatening. Not that it's a good thing as they can hardly keep tracking the amulet while lugging a cataleptic dog. Or should that be dogaleptic?

"Zane, can you take him back to the restaurant? I'd take him, but I'm worried I might lose track of the amulet." Frankie can tell it's still nearby, but this isn't to say it'll remain there.

The Nautilus doesn't look happy about leaving her alone with Dominik. However, he doesn't hesitate to bend down, scoop up Dex and disappear a second later.

"Do not fret Ta ha zemrën, I will take care of you," whispers Dominik into her ear. His breath is warm on her neck and it's not unpleasant, at all. He'll take care of her? She's tempted to put him on the ground, but isn't sure she can do so without using her magic.

Thoughts of sitting atop him, flood her mind, bringing a smile to her lips. She's just got her tinfoil beanie back in place when Zane pops up next to her.

Frankie immediately takes a big step back, distancing herself from the vampire. She then has to fight to shift her expression into neutral. *"Wow, you were quick. What d'you do, just chuck Dex at Sophie and come back?"* Part of her is slightly peeved. Who is it he doesn't trust, her or Dominik?

"You I trust. Him? Hell no."

Okay, so that answers that question. "Shall we get on with it?" Rather than ask this question telepathically, Frankie says it out loud, thereby including the vampire. She gets brief nods of acceptance from both men.

"We move in slowly, and no eating any cake."

As the smallest, Frankie is the first to sneak her head through the palms that crowd the corner of the building. Zane soon towers over her, his head right above hers. Meantime, Dominik has squeezed in next to her. All three of them spot the bizarre set up at the same time. Rather than move forward, they back up and regroup.

Zane is not amused. There's no need for Frankie to use her vampire super powers to know this. His expression as he looks at Dominik is thunderous. "I thought you said you searched over here?"

Dominik bristles, pulling himself up to his full height. This has him looking down on Zane and Frankie can tell it doesn't sit well with her merman boyfriend.

"You honestly think I'd miss something like that?" Dominik throws his hand in the general direction of the tea party. "Seriously?"

As angry as Dominik appears, it's a miracle his voice hasn't risen above a hissed whisper. If Zane had questioned her like this, she suspects she'd now be yelling at him. Okay, so telepathically, but still.

Not keen on playing the part of devil's advocate, Frankie has no option if she's going to stop them coming to blows. *"He does have a point. He would've reported on something as weird as that."*

Zane's shoulders drop and he nods slowly. He knows she's right, he just doesn't like it.

Again the three of them peer around the corner of the building. Frankie allows her senses to expand and suspects Dominik is doing the same.

"There's no-one there," they say in concert.

Even this small show of unity has Zane frowning. He really does need to get over himself.

Without the fear of running into anyone, the three of them walk casually around the corner. Standing abreast, they survey what's in front of them. It truly is like some weird mad hatter's tea party. There's a long wooden table covered in a white, lace table cloth. There's nothing picnic about the crockery, either.

Dotted along the table are stacked cake plates with each layer jam-packed with pastries and other goodies. Thank goodness Dex is back at the restaurant. On seeing this lot there'd have been no holding him back. Even Frankie is tempted.

If it hadn't been for Dex proving the cake is real, Frankie would suspect she was looking at a mirage. She walks over to the table and touches one of the large teapots. This has her pulling her hand back sharply. It's hot, as though it's just been filled.

As traps go, it's more than a little obvious. The one thing missing is a huge cardboard box, a stick and a piece of string. What's also missing is the signature of the amulet. Even closing her eyes and stretching her arms out to the side, Frankie's no longer able to detect it.

Bejinxed bunnies! Whoever had it must have moved while she was transfixed by the high-end afternoon tea. "It's gone. I can't sense the amulet anymore."

Something else that disappears a second later is the whole tea party, with not so much as a crumb left behind. Frankie knows she isn't responsible and Zane shaking his head takes him out of the running too. All that's left is a cloud of residual magic where the table had stood. Frankie walks through it in hopes of getting a lead on the witch or warlock responsible.

"It's the same as I detected at the bottom of the cliff."

In some ways the magic's as familiar to Frankie as if it were her own. However, it's the overtones of pure evil that have her shaking herself free of its embrace. She looks down at the dried grass. "I searched this part of the resort when I was on top of the hill. I didn't pick up anyone, magical or otherwise."

Dominik's in agreement, nodding in a measured way. "I didn't distinguish anything when I was here earlier, either."

Frankie shakes her head to center her thoughts. Even if the magical signature is different, it doesn't necessarily rule out the obvious suspect. "It's gotta be Calico Jack. Who else could it be?"

Frankie isn't expecting an answer, and she doesn't get one. Instead she gets a question.

Zane, who's deep in thought, doesn't even bother to look at her when he speaks. "What if it was the guy by the cliff that set this up? Dex smelled cake on his hand, didn't he?"

Frankie admits he's got a point, there's one problem with his theory. "I'd agree with you, but that dude was human through-and-through. There was nothing magical about him. He's also rather dead, so how could he make the tea party disappear like it just did?"

Dominik scuffs the ground where the table had once stood. "I'm a vampire, and yet I have friends who are witches." Not once during this statement do his eyes leave Frankie.

7

Frankie looks from Dominik to Zane. "There's one way to be sure." Much as she's loath to search out her grandparents, it's going to be the quickest way to find out if they set the trap, and why. The more Frankie thinks on it, the less likely it is that the trap was for her and the others.

She puts her hand gently on the vampire's shoulder to lessen the blow of her words. "Dominik, you head back to the restaurant and we'll see you there later."

Frankie dealing with her grandparents is going to be a big enough challenge. There's no way she's doing so to a background of these two flinging chunks of testosterone at each other.

Dominik is digging his toes in when, without warning, Zane whips his wand out. "Allow me." A moment later the Nautilus disappears taking the vampire with him.

He's back in a blink and chuckling away.

"Right, let's get out of here, before he comes back. He's fast, I'll give him that."

Zane doesn't bother putting his wand away. Instead he pulls Frankie into a tight embrace and waves it around them. This sees them standing, and once again visible, audible and sniffable, on the deck of the jungle villa. A stunned Anne and Calico Jack sit at the table in front of them.

Before her grandparents can berate them for turning up without an invitation, Frankie holds her hand up. "Hear us out."

As requested, they both stay silent, with Calico Jack even indicating they can take a seat. They do so and Frankie's further surprised by cold drinks appearing in front of them. As thirsty as she suddenly is, there's no way she's drinking it. Something she conveys to Zane telepathically, and that sees him also leaving his glass untouched.

Frankie doesn't bother looking at Anne Bonny when she asks her question. The woman's main power is her ability to steal stuff and be obnoxious while doing so. Instead she looks at her granddad. "Do you know anything about the mad hatter's tea party down at the resort?"

Frankie doesn't need him to respond verbally. She can tell by his befuddled expression that he doesn't have a clue what she's on about.

Anne slaps the table top to get Frankie's attention away from that of her partner. "The what? The mad hatter's tea party you say?"

Yep, totally obnoxious.

Frankie runs through what it was they'd stumbled upon, drawing incredulous looks from the pair of them. She knows they're not *this* good at acting. And it's this that has her picking up her glass for a sip. She's about to, when her senses and her tummy tingle. She puts it back down again.

The sneaky ratbag.

Zane picks up his own glass. Her warning of, *"Drink that and you'll be out cold in seconds,"* has him putting it back down and even moving it to one side.

She has no idea why Jack would want to drug them other than to stop them searching for treasure. Frankie whips out her wand, with Calico Jack following suit. It's an old-fashioned magical standoff. Her free hand, Frankie throws up a ward courtesy of her weird combo powers. This is backed up by something from Zane. The pair is as good as bullet-proof, and certainly hex-proof.

"Why did you try to drug us? We already told you we're here on holiday." Frankie waits, interested to see if Dominik has truly altered their memories as he's said.

Calico Jack sighs deeply before responding. "You turning up like this, I thought you might be in cahoots with your Aunt Betty. Never did like the woman. Blasted goody two-shoes, she is. You're a lot like her, really."

Frankie straightens in her seat. She's just been insulted by being compared to someone who's nice. Okay, she can live with that. Anne sneering at mention of her mysterious aunt also makes the missing relative okay by Frankie. Of more interest is that neither her dad nor Nana Peg has mentioned an Aunt Betty. How come CJ knows about her? "I've got an Aunt Betty?"

"You have, my sister. Not that I've seen the woman in decades. Disappeared without a by your leave. Typical she'd turn up right when we're about to..."

A loud thump comes from under the table and Frankie suspects Anne has just put the boot in. This is interesting. Frankie's torn as to what to quiz him on first. His sister disappearing without trace and turning up seemingly out of the blue are enthralling. There's even the mystery of what's about to happen, although Frankie suspects she knows what that is. What intrigues Frankie is far more down to earth than any of these.

"You have a sister?"

She hasn't read anything about a sister in the history books. Still, if the ghost of Captain Garnet is to be believed, those volumes aren't overly accurate. If CJ's sister is as squeaky clean as he's saying, it would make sense that she's stayed below the radar.

"Hang on, if she's a paragon of virtue, why is she trying to drug people?"

"Not people, us." Calico Jack points to himself and then Anne.

"Why's that?" Sure Frankie's got a few ideas, but she's learned never to assume when it comes to members of the magical community. Whether Calico Jack is going to come clean, or tell porkies, who knows?

He looks skyward, breathing out heavily before looking Frankie in the eye. She could almost believe he's going to tell her the truth.

"She wants Anne and me to get hitched. I'm thinking what you saw is her idea of a wedding breakfast. She doesn't agree with us 'living in sin' as she puts it."

That he even finger quotes 'living in sin' has Frankie grinning. Does she think he's telling her the truth? Heck no. Well, not if the expressions on Anne's face have been any indicator. These have gone from surprised, to delighted before finishing up with fuming. Frankie doesn't know what to make of it. Could it be her unbearable grandmamma has hopes of Calico Jack 'putting a ring on it'?

"What does she look like?"

Zane has asked the very question Frankie had

been about to. Far better they have an idea so they can avoid her if they have to. Sure Calico Jack has spun a story of a mysterious aunt roaming around trying for a shotgun wedding. This could be a complete fabrication on his part, with approaching the woman proving injurious to their health. Frankie wouldn't put it past her granddad to stitch her up by getting them ensnared in a trap meant for him.

Calico Jack waves his wand in the air, creating a shimmering panel of light, similar to a home theatre. Safe behind their double shield of protection, Zane and Frankie watch the movie he plays for them. All that's missing is a bucket of popcorn.

The credits don't even have time to roll before Frankie's had enough. She knows a hoax when she sees one. The way CJ paints it, Frankie's Aunt Betty could give Mother Theresa a run for her money. While she's sure the woman is very nice, Frankie's not this gullible.

"Well that's great. We'll keep an eye out for her. And yes," Frankie holds her hand up to forestall the protest from both grandparents, "your location is safe with us."

Rather than transport themselves back to the restaurant magically, Frankie and Zane leave the jungle villa on foot. Only when they're out of earshot, do they slow.

Frankie waits for Zane to reinstate the cloaking spell before she speaks. "Well this could explain why the magic feels familiar to me. If he's telling the truth, I'm related to the witch responsible. As to that baloney about her wanting them to get hitched, I'm not buying it."

Zane pulls some vines out of the way and stands to the side. "Me neither. Did you also notice your Aunt Betty had more than a passing resemblance to Betty White?"

Frankie scoots past him and takes the lead although she stops soon after. "I knew she looked familiar! But, not even Betty White is as saintly as my granddad is making my aunt out to be. I'm amazed she wasn't sporting a halo in that home movie of his."

"Do you think she actually exists? Or does her invention simply suit Calico Jack and Anne's needs?"

Frankie thinks on it for a beat. "If the energy I've picked up is to be believed, she exists alright, and we're sure as Hades related. Fingers crossed she's nothing like those two." Frankie hooks her thumb back in the direction of the jungle villa. Unfortunately the tinges of evil that had lingered at the former site of the tea party say otherwise.

They're striding along the jungle trail when Frankie stops so suddenly, Zane canons into her. This has them sprawling into the undergrowth in a jumble of arms and legs.

They eventually untangle themselves, and Zane puts his hands gently on either side of

Frankie's face, holding her still. "What happened? What's wrong? Are you okay?"

Frankie covers his hands with hers and squeezes them in reassurance.

"I'm fine. It's just that I picked up on something that's missing from Calico Jack's story.

"What's that?"

"My Aunt Betty. Sure I've sensed her magic, but I didn't pick up on the woman herself when I scanned the island earlier."

"That doesn't make sense. How can you pick up on her magical signature if she's not actually here?"

The only conclusion they can come up with is that the woman is coming and going from the island. As to where she's off to, who knows?

They continue on to the restaurant, keeping a wary eye out for any of the imperial guard, the Garnets, and even Frankie's mysterious aunt. They don't come across anyone. The resort is as good as deserted. There aren't even any parrots in residence in the palm trees that dot the place.

Frankie rubs her hands up and down her arms, smoothing goosebumps that have no place showing up in the tropics. "I don't like how quiet it is." It's this that has her holding her wand soon after.

Zane is also armed. "You're right. There's something wrong. Can you sense anything?"

Hexed halibut, Frankie keeps forgetting she

can search for inconsistences. "Hold up. I can't do the searching thingee and walk at the same time."

To Frankie it would be as tricky as patting her head and rubbing her tummy. Sure once she's locked onto the energy, she can move. It's the linking to it in the first place that's tricky.

To avoid any nasty surprises, the pair stands back-to-back. This time she doesn't close her eyes. No point finding the trace and then being thumped because it's right in front of you. Or should that be 'they're' right in front of you?

It's interesting, that with her eyes open she can actually see her energy leave her body and spread out across the resort. She can even see when it picks something up, with the sensation flooding her body a second later. "I've picked someone up. I think it might be my Aunt Betty."

"How do you know that?"

"Earl Grey tea, scones oh and a tinge of malice."

"No way? You mean to say Calico Jack was telling the truth?" Zane's skepticism is back in full force.

On the face of it, this would appear to be the case. Even so, Frankie isn't planning on striding up to her aunt and giving her a big ol' hug. Sure if CJ and Anne don't like her, chances are she's okay. But you know what they say about 'assume'. She also doesn't like the malevolence that helps make up the woman's magical signature.

"Let's go say hello to dear old Betty." Frankie then throws wards up around herself and Zane. He does the same, double coating them in magical protection.

"Mom, are you okay? You've been gone aaaaages."

"Dex, I'm fine, but I am going to be a little longer. How are you feeling?

Despite her not picking up on anything when he keeled over, she wants to check there are no lasting effects from him being drugged.

"I'm good. Sophie made me some more sandwiches."

And just like that the world rights itself on its axis. If he's wolfing down food, there can't be too much wrong with him. *"Okay then. You be a good pup and guard the others."*

His telepathic *'Grrrr'* is loud in her head, letting her know he's already assumed his attack pose. Better he's on duty there than underfoot when she meets the latest member of her family. You just never knew what you were going to get with her rellies.

They're back near the scene of the tea party when Frankie slows her steps, finally stopping. Zane pulls up next to her. The energy emanating from her aunt is as good as solid. Frankie even reaches out fully expecting to be able to grab handfuls of the stuff. That's weird; she can't even penetrate the wall of energy. Not that she's keen on doing so. It might even be this very barrier that's stopped Frankie from detecting her aunt's mortal form from atop the hill.

She backs up, her finger to her lips. Zane's eyes narrow, mystified as to why she's retreating. It's not something she does often, but it's what she's going to do now. Only once they're a few feet back from the invisible force field, does Frankie wave her wand around them. This sees them as far from her relative as the resort allows, without a machete being involved.

"What the heck?" Zane looks at her and scratches his head. "She can't be that poisonous, can she?"

"Her energy, it's definitely the same as that I felt at the cliff face, and by the tea party."

"Do you think she was responsible for the rock slide?"

"I don't think so. From what I saw, the cliff face collapsing was an accident. But the amulet being taken from his still-warm hand? Now that was on purpose."

"Perhaps the amulet is hers?"

Frankie fingers her own on its chain around her neck. "You could be right." While Frankie and Anne's amulets have been jinxed to stop them being removed, this isn't to say all amulets are protected this way.

Zane slings his arm around Frankie's shoulders. "Let's go back to the restaurant. I'm hanging out for a drink that won't see me comatose."

"You got that right. We also need to get our heads around where we go from here because we are way off plan right now."

Not once in their session at *Magic Beans* had there been any contingency for all the scenarios they've encountered. Finding out the imperial guards and William are staying at the resort. A dead guy camped out at the cliff face. A new, and potentially dangerous, relation. Add to this a possible family wedding, and things are getting way more complicated by the second.

They don't simply march into the courtyard out front of the restaurant. Even though they're back to being invisible, any guards with their wits about them will pick up someone is passing by. It's also safer for them to enter through the front doors than simply appear in the middle of the restaurant. The team being on high alert, they could be fanged or zapped before they have a chance to announce themselves.

Sure enough, the imperial guards, and even William, are sitting around in the courtyard. None of them have cold drinks which, given the heat, says the restaurant is still out of bounds. It's something that doesn't make sense to Frankie. Surely there are mini bars in each of the high-end villas that dot the property? It's not as if the guards will be stung mini bar prices, so why not help themselves?

"I've just thought of something?"

Zane raises an eyebrow. "You mind sharing?"

"Why aren't they getting drinks from the mini bars in the villas?"

While a small mystery — or should that be mini — it's one they can solve by checking out the nearest villa. Even if it's one of the cheaper units due to the night-time noise from the restaurant, it should still have a mini bar.

It does.

"This doesn't make sense. If the guards and William are so blinkin' thirsty, why not help themselves to these?" Frankie removes a small bottle of bubbles, holding it up for Zane to see. "It's the good stuff too."

She eases the cork out, making sure not to create a loud 'pop' in the process. A quick sniff and she allows her senses to expand, checking out the bubbles and the other drinks in the small fridge. No wonder the guards don't want a bar of the mini bars. If they were to drink anything in here, they'd be out cold.

Zane sniffs the bottle she hands to him. "Well that explains that, then."

"Yep. The question is, do the guards know about the sleeping potion from experience, or are they in on it?"

Zane empties the small bottle of bubbles down the sink. "If it's because they've been drugged themselves, it must be your aunt who's behind it."

Frankie closes the small fridge. "It could be anyone magical."

"The other thing we have to ask ourselves is why whoever it is doesn't want to kill everyone straight off? Why bother drugging them and then killing them by pegging them out on the beach?"

Zane's right, it doesn't make sense. From what her Nana Peg says, the Wereall concentrate on locking up those who are guilty. William is the exception to this. He's pay-to-stay all the way without a care whether the inmate is innocent or guilty. "Could the spiked drinks be how the Garnet family traps their business rivals?"

Even without him nodding, she can tell Zane agrees with her.

Frankie presses on with her theory. "It would be the easiest way to get the guests from here through to *All Hallows Keep* without them putting up a fight."

"We need to speak to the others about this, Shortcake." Zane smiles broadly before continuing. "Fancy creating a diversion that'll empty the courtyard by the restaurant?"

8

Frankie stands in the courtyard out front of the restaurant with Zane. It's now a Wereall-free zone. "That was spectacular!"

"Yeah, for small bottles, they sure made a lot of noise."

Frankie already has her hand on the doors to the restaurant before she replies. "And less chance of anyone being drugged by accident."

It had been her idea to have the bottles of bubbles in the mini fridges exploding, their joint incantation a thing of beauty. As well as clearing the resultant courtyard, the noise will have given her aunt a rev up too. Better the old girl is concentrating on their high-end French 'explosives', than bothering Frankie and her friends.

Frankie doesn't want to lose sight of their ultimate mission to free the innocent. And every time they run into another obstacle, they're further delayed. It's something that's nibbling at Frankie's psyche and not in a good way.

She swings the doors wide and enters the restaurant with Zane hot on her heels and singing out their arrival. "We're home!"

The reactions of the team range from delighted, to down-right terrified. Dex is thrilled to have his mom home in one piece while Dominik looks to still be annoyed Zane got rid of him earlier. Luca and Magda, although still close together on the sofa, aren't as loved-up as earlier.

Meantime Nana Peg is sitting in a corner rocking slowly, with Sophie doing her best to reassure the Wereall she's safe.

Frankie walks over to see what's up with her nana, although it's Sophie she addresses. "It wasn't that loud, was it?"

"Not the explosions outside," hisses Luca. "But, when that lot went off, it was like being back in WWII." He stabs his finger toward the fridge at the end of the row.

The safety glass in the door is cracked and glazed, with foam running down the inside in clouds. Frankie's horrified at the damage she and Zane have done.

"I'm so sorry. I didn't think there would be any mini bottles in here." On their arrival, she like the others had been more interested in juice or water. She hadn't been looking for champagne.

Zane's eyebrows are draw together in concentration. He holds onto this expression a second before speaking. "This makes no sense. The wards we've got in place should have stopped our spell from reaching these fridges."

Sophie looks up from comforting Nana Peg. "The wards you've got in place, what sort of magic are they designed to repel?"

Frankie doesn't answer, neither does Zane. The small witch simply asking has let them know where they've messed up. It's Zane who answers Sophie first.

"Straight witch magic, that's what the wards are designed for."

"But that's not what I used to set the bottles off," says Frankie, even if there's no need.

No sooner has she finished speaking than she grabs her wand and sets about putting more wards in place. Zane joins her.

This time they throw every kind of power swirling in their systems at these layers of protection. Frankie even ensures CJ and Anne won't be able to simply stroll into the place like they had earlier.

Whether the wards are good enough to keep her Aunt Betty at bay, the Goddess knows. The woman's magical signature still has Frankie scratching her head. There's something decidedly off about it.

Zane and Frankie help themselves to cold

drinks from a still intact fridge before dropping into the sofa they'd shared earlier.

Nana Peg, who's been coaxed out of her corner by Sophie, appears confused by Frankie's mention of an Aunt Betty. "I know of no relation of this name."

Zane holds his half empty bottle against his forehead, rolling it back and forth. "She's Calico Jack's sister, apparently."

"That makes her a full-blooded witch," adds Frankie, helpfully. In other words she's not hairy, although Frankie keeps this thought to herself.

"This explains it." Nana Peg absently scratches behind her ear before continuing. "I've not met anyone from his side of the family. The one who traveled to the world of the Wereall escaped well before my time."

Frankie looks at each of the group in turn. "The problem we've got is where we go from here." There's no need for her to explain that their original plan is toast. A wave of her wand and there's a whiteboard standing in front of the restaurant's double doors. There are colored markers along the ledge at its base. Things are way beyond using a single black marker.

The front and back of the whiteboard are crowded with scribbles and flow charts before the team is happy with their revised plan.

One thing's for sure, they daren't stay any longer at the resort. No point giving William and his guards the chance to scupper their new plan. And who knows what Aunt Betty's agenda is, because Frankie isn't buying the wedding angle. There's something about the woman's magic that has the hairs on the back of Frankie's neck sticking out like uncooked spaghetti.

Sure they need to find a murderer, but this will have to wait until they get back from *All Hallows Keep*.

Because of the Wereall Empire running to its own timetable, it doesn't matter when they go through the rock face. Chances are the time will be different when they've passed through to the other side.

Frankie puts the red whiteboard marker back on the ledge and looks at everyone in turn. "As nice as it would be to tidy up here first, it isn't an option. For all we know, a couple of days here could feel like ten years to those inmates." It could also feel like ten seconds, but it's a risk Frankie's not willing to take.

She looks out the window at the setting sun. It's early by Seattle standards, but they are in the tropics. "Let's spend the night on the *Pearl*. We can go through to the keep first thing in the morning when we're rested."

Frankie also doubts her Nana Peg is up to facing any action right now. She's stopped rocking, but that's about it. At the slightest movement by any of the team, the woman's hackles spring to attention. She's more flight than fight and it's something they definitely don't need.

The group stands in a circle, with Dex hanging over Frankie's left shoulder like she's about to burp him. Her other arm is wrapped tightly around her Nana Peg making her conscious of the woman trembling in waves. Zane then takes the group back to the schooner, landing them neatly on the deck.

Once there, Zane takes Dex off Frankie's shoulder and puts him down on the deck. Frankie's free to drag her nana in for a tight embrace, running her hand up and down the woman's back in a soothing motion. On realizing this is rubbing the woman's fur up the wrong way she stops immediately. "Are you sure you'll be okay?"

There's nothing emphatic about the nod against Frankie's shoulder. This surprises her. Aren't the Wereall supposed to be stronger in their totem form? If this is true Peggy must be the most timid human on the planet when she takes that shape. It's something to be aware of moving forward. After showing Peggy to her cabin and checking she's got everything she needs, Frankie heads for her own. Sure it's early, but she's more than ready for bed.

The best thing about spending the night on the *Pearl* is there's not a chance William and his crew will find them. As to her Aunt Betty, who knows? Frankie's unsure on a couple of levels. And is her aunt to be trusted? Or is her aunt in cahoots with William, the Garnets, or both? It's something that has her throwing up protection spells until it's as though the schooner floats in a large bubble.

Frankie is woken the next morning by Dex hounding her to open their cabin door. Still half asleep it takes a second to understand his urgency. He can't have need of the bathroom. Not after she'd had to take him to the island for a pit stop at four that morning.

Frankie sniffs the air as hard as Dex is doing. She knows if they don't hurry, there'll be nothing left. That is unless Nana Peg has made the muffins. Then there'll be plenty left behind, with most of it on the walls, floor and even the ceiling.

A quick visit to the bathroom and a wave of her wand, and Frankie is washed and dressed.

"Hurry up, Mom. I can smell their saliva."

"Okay, okay. If they've all gone when we get out there, I'll magic up some more for you."

Frankie opens the cabin door and follows Dex along the narrow corridor. Even before she gets to the kitchen, she knows they're too late. Her familiar's howls of anguish are testimony to this. Good thing she's brought her wand with her. Actually it never leaves her side now, especially not when they're in what she's thinking of as enemy territory.

She doesn't bother entering the galley, knowing it'll be packed with bodies, and a few stray crumbs. A wave of her silver wand and Dex's tune changes from despair to delight. She's even made sure there are a couple of muffins at ground level so he can get stuck straight in. While it might not be the best to feed the small pup this much sugar, he's going to need the energy.

So is she, and it's this that has her waving her wand again. This time the baked goods don't arrive in the galley. She's holding a double chocolate chip muffin the size of a small child's head. Frankie stuffs her wand in the pocket of her shorts and gets stuck in.

She's really filling her face when Zane steps out of the small kitchen. On seeing what she's up to, he breaks into a broad grin. "I tried saving some for you, but I was in danger of losing a hand."

Her mouth is too full to answer him verbally. Instead she replies telepathically, trying her best not to mumble. *"No worries, I don't think chocolate was on the menu, anyway. I could kill for a coffee though."*

"As you wish."

A snap of his fingers and he's holding a go-cup. The briefest sniff and she's sure it's a cup of *Magic Beans'* finest. She stuffs the last of the muffin in her mouth, grabs the coffee and takes a tentative sip. Yep, coffee this smooth has to be courtesy of Mac at *Magic Beans*.

Frankie hadn't realized Mac does takeaway coffees. Good to know although pointless once they cross over to the realm of the Wereall. That place is lost in space and time, making it the perfect location for a prison for magical beings.

Frankie takes another sip of coffee, savoring it as she swallows. "Is everyone ready to go?"

"Pretty much. Nana Peg's still on edge after the fridge exploding though."

This could be an issue. If it wasn't for Frankie's Wereall relation knowing her way around inside the keep, she could stay here. As it is, she's an integral part of their plan.

Sophie is the next to leave the small galley kitchen, with Stinky stuffed down her cleavage as usual. "I'm thinking there might be something I can give her to calm her down."

Frankie nods her agreement to this. She then

remembers Sophie's propensity to go overboard. "Just calm her down, though. No having her stoned out of her gourd. She won't be any good to us if she's like that."

"I was thinking a smidge of St John's Wort. It'll take the edge off, but she'll still be able to function."

Both Frankie and Zane voice their approval to this.

"I'll be right back." Sophie waves her wand above her head and disappears. That the small witch has used her wand says the drug of choice isn't stowed in her cabin. Perhaps it's at the restaurant. Frankie hasn't decided when Sophie returns. "That Dr Marvin, he's such a sweetheart." That the small witch is blushing furiously points to her having a sweet spot for the medical warlock.

"I'll just go give these to Peggy." The coven's healer/bomb expert walks back into the galley, leaving Frankie and Zane on their own in the corridor.

Frankie isn't in agreement with Sophie about Marvin the Magnificent. The esteemed doctor had been as good as useless when Zane was put into a death-like coma. Frankie suspects Beatrice his rabbit could have achieved as much. And she's cuter too.

"Be careful with your thoughts, Frankie.

Marvin is renowned for hearing EVERYTHING, especially if it's about him."

Frankie concentrates on cloaking her mind before she responds. "I thought he had to be nearby for that to happen?"

Zane shakes his head slowly. She'd think he was deadly serious if it wasn't for the twinkle in his bright blue eyes.

"Sheesh, are the contents of my mind safe at all?" The idea that the glorified vaudeville performer can listen into all her thoughts isn't a happy one.

"You just need to protect your mind better, even if I enjoy listening in from time to time. It lets me know where I stand."

Zane lips are a hairsbreadth away from her ear when he whispers the last few words to her. She's going all gooey when she recalls some thoughts she's had about him. Now she's blushing as madly as Sophie had been earlier. Maybe she needs to invest in an actual tinfoil beanie because obviously the virtual one is failing miserably?

Zane presses his lips to her forehead before speaking to her telepathically. *"Don't stop on my account. I love that it brings us closer."*

9

Rather than travel directly to the cliff face from the *Pearl*, the group returns to the restaurant, careful to materialize inside. A quick look out the double doors and Frankie's surprised to see the courtyard is empty. Surely William and his imperial guard haven't given up this easily. She's also amazed her missing Aunt Betty isn't out there, waiting with wedding invitations in hand.

The first thing they do is unload all the containers. Backpacks are handed to each of the team, and even Dex gets allocated little saddlebags. Frankie isn't keen on him having access to explosives, knowing how much trouble the pup can get into. But, it's been decided if anyone is running low, he's got the best chance of getting through to them.

Again it's all about rum ball explosives with Sophie. After stowing her own bag-full of charges in her backpack, Frankie looks up to find Zane grinning. She's wondering what he's so happy about until she follows his gaze.

"Dominik! Don't eat that!" Frankie's voice is loud enough that even she winces.

She frowns at Zane before walking over to take the rum ball out of the vampire's hand. When she explains how lethal the small chocolate ball is, Dominik joins her in glaring at Zane. She pops the confectionery in the paper bag in his other hand and marches over to Zane's side.

"That wasn't funny. What if he'd actually bitten down on it? A headless vampire won't be much help to us, will he?"

"I wouldn't worry too much about that one. Knowing my luck his head would grow back."

Much as Frankie would like to grill Zane on this, they need to get to the cliff face sooner rather than later. They've already wasted enough time. Every delay however small is like having ants crawling under her skin. She's scratching her arm again when Nana Peg walks over and steers Frankie into the kitchen. It's the first time the woman has willingly approached her.

And if this wasn't enough, her nana runs her hand over the scratches on Frankie's forearm. The crawling sensation is immediately soothed. "I hadn't expected someone with so little Wereall blood to react as badly. Of course, your blood isn't the same as others."

Wow, that's like over twenty words. In a row! Frankie waits for her nana to continue, something the woman does eventually. However, the wait has been long enough that Frankie finds herself scratching her other arm.

"Your heritage is what's got you reacting as you are. Your knowing there are innocents locked up at the keep bothers you greatly, doesn't it?"

Frankie forces herself to stop scratching, worried she's going to scar herself for life if she keeps it up. "My thoughts of them being stuck there are deafening. But, I'm still worried we'll accidentally release someone who's supposed to be locked up."

Rather than answer her immediate concerns, Nana Peg runs her hands down both of Frankie's arms. It's as though her nana has smeared her arms with aloe, so instant is the relief. Shame it doesn't last.

"When the time comes, you'll know who should be released. It's in your blood, child."

Despite Frankie's nagging, Nana Peg won't be drawn further on her whole "when the time comes" and "it's in your blood" predictions. Frankie's as in the dark as ever and can only hope her nana is right. If she's not, the world is about to be overrun with evil the likes of which it's never seen before. If Frankie could ignore the innocent and carry on with her life, she would. Unfortunately she suspects doing so would have her clawing herself to shreds.

Less than half an hour following her nana's pep talk and they're ready to go. Each member of the team including Stinky and Dex has welding goggles atop their heads. These can be pulled down in seconds preventing them from being blinded by Sophie's flash charges.

It's seeing what the vampires are wearing that brings Frankie up short. They're dressed from head to toe in unforgiving black leather. Frankie suspects that vampires alone could get away with the look. Basically unless you're hot and in great shape, you'd end up resembling something seen hanging in a deli. Dominik in particular looks mouth-watering, and darn if he doesn't know it.

Putting their model-hot looks to one side, perhaps the most startling feature of the outfits is the breast plates. These carry a shield featuring a wolf and an eagle in a fight to the death. It's not easy to make this out with the matt black metal of the breast plate all but swallowed up the relief.

Frankie taps Magda's shield. "I guess that's one way to stop someone shoving a stake through your heart. Aren't you gonna be hot though?"

Magda runs her hand down the piece of metal lovingly. "Being 'ot is better than being dead."

Frankie isn't sure about this. It's one thing to be dressed like that while in the air-conditioned comfort of the restaurant. Once they leave for the cliff face, the vampires will be sweating harder than the island's resident pigs. That's if they even sweat. It's not something Frankie has thought of before now.

By comparison, the witches and Nana Peg look as if they're on their way to a picnic. It isn't that they're going through to *All Hallows Keep* dressed as they are. No, Frankie, Zane and Sophie will be taking care of costume changes before this happens. Until such time they may as well be comfortable.

Dex sits at Luca's feet and looks up in awe. *"Mom, why can't I wear my new outfit?"*

It's no secret the Jack Russell is thrilled with his new leather coat, especially after she added all the extra studs he deemed necessary. She's a little worried that with full saddlebags he won't be able to stand, let alone walk.

"Not a chance, Dex. I am not having you whining about being hot. You'll just have to wait."

Once everyone's ready, including a blissed-out Nana Peg, they link together for the trip to the cliff face. First though, Frankie double checks they won't arrive to any nasty shocks. Nope, the way is clear.

A brief wave of her wand and a second later the group stands in front of the wall of rock. The first thing Frankie notices is there's no longer a hand sticking out the pile of rocks at the bottom of the cliff face. While this development is interesting, she's not going to let it distract her. Dex is halfway up the pile when she yells at him to get back to her side. Blast him and his sugar addiction.

Her familiar safely at her ankles, Frankie points her wand at the pile of rocks moving it swiftly to one side. This will reveal the runes, allowing her to point her amulet at them, thus opening the rock face.

Only problem is the runes aren't where she'd etched them on her last visit. They must have been removed when the cliff collapsed.

Thoughts of what she'd seen through the eyes of the dead guy have her stepping back. It's something she encourages the others to do too. Their having seen how large the pile of rocks she'd shifted had been, none of them put forward any arguments. Not even Dex.

Unsure if her amulet can open the rock face with the runes no longer there, Frankie still has to try. In readiness for the cliff opening, she holds her wand in her right hand ready for a rapid change of wardrobe. She knows from experience the chasm doesn't stay open long and stragglers run the risk of being squished. She then takes her amulet from her top with her left hand and points it at the cliff. Last time she'd done this, a stream of light had shot out and locked onto the runes. This time there's nothing.

She points it in another direction, then another and another. Still nothing happens, even after she tries flipping it over. Great, she's back to being powerless again. It doesn't sit well. "Houston, we have a problem."

Zane steps up to her side. "Maybe try a reversal of the incantation you used to seal the place."

"I'm not sure. My gut is telling me this entrance is a bust."

As to why, the possibilities are endless. With William and his goons running amok over the island it could well be them. Then there's Frankie's aunt to consider. Who knows what her agenda is. As to Calico Jack and Anne, Frankie doubts it's them. They're more interested in digging up treasure than gaining access to the realm of the Wereall.

Unless that is, there's treasure somewhere in the keep? Would William be the type to hoard gold and precious gems?

"That would be a yes. No doubt taken from the inmates."

Zane answering her has her berating herself again for her errant thoughts. Only when she's finished does she add CJ and Anne to the list of those likely to have tampered with the runes on the cliff. Both of them are in possession of amulets similar to hers.

Nana Peg steps forward; on Frankie's other side. "This is exactly what happened when I tried to go home. My amulet would light up, but nothing happened."

Frankie still isn't sure why her nana was in the human world in her Wereall form when Frankie locked the portal. She'd love to ask, but somehow it feels too personal.

Frankie looks at her Wereall relation. "Hah, I can't even get mine to light up."

"What if you combined the power of your amulets?"

This suggestion from Zane has Frankie and Nana Peg staring at him and then each other. The Wereall's face being covered in hair; it's a little tricky to read her expression. Her gaze, however, appear hopeful.

Frankie grabs hold of her amulet again. "Shall we?"

A moment later and Nana Peg is similarly armed. As one, they turn to face the cliff.

This time Frankie's amulet lights up. Oh boy, does it light up. The one thing not going up is the cliff face. Huge chunks rain down on the ground in front of them causing them to stumble backward. The resultant cloud of dust and debris has everyone pulling their goggles down into place. Even Dex manages to pull his down with a paw.

Eventually the dust clears. Rather than be faced with a chasm in the rock, they're looking at a rock face that's as solid as it was before the collapse. Nothing to lose, Frankie tries a reversal of the spell that had locked the cliff when they'd left last time. Again nothing happens apart from more rock breaking away and landing on the ground in front of them.

What had been a pristine section of jungle now has more in common with an open pit mine. Frankie turns her back on her latest failure, shrugging at the three vampires who've kept back and quiet. "We're gonna need to find another way in."

"The guards, we follow them?" suggests Magda.

Luca squeezes Magda's shoulders in support of her suggestion before adding one of his own. "This William, he obviously got through to the island somehow."

They're right of course. Perhaps it's that she's too ready to think of William and his guards being here because of a failed spell of hers?

Sophie coughs to clear her throat of dust before speaking. "Could it be they're back there now? I was expecting to see them camped out in the courtyard again."

"And yet, they weren't." Frankie says this to herself as much as the group at large. "Come on, everyone touching."

She doesn't need to hurry them along, with the group in a huddle soon after. A wave of Zane's wand and they're back at the restaurant. It isn't that they need more supplies. It's that this is a safe place to arrive as a group. They also won't arrive in the middle of the imperial guard, or anyone else. If she hadn't sensed her aunt on a couple of occasions, Frankie would think Betty a figment of CJ's fertile imagination.

They don't linger at the restaurant any longer than it takes to throw back cold drinks to clear the last of the rock dust from their throats.

"Okay," Frankie looks around the group, making eye contact with each of them, "we're on foot from here. Keep your eyes open for any hint of William and the imperial guards."

Even though she knows the team doesn't need to be reminded, she can't help repeating their mission statement. She knows from experience that if things get hairy, it's all too easy to lose sight of your goal.

Following another night aboard the *Pearl*, they return to the restaurant after breakfast. Once there the three vampires, Zane, Frankie and even Sophie and Dex, go through their set moves. In the interests of safety, Sophie uses tennis balls to replicate her charges.

After a cool down, they leave in twos and threes on the search for another portal. Despite seeing a number of imperial guards and following them, their targets aren't going anywhere. Other than circling the resort on an hourly basis that is. And if they're not going anywhere, there's no point following them.

It's something that's decided after Magda and Luca had followed a pair in circles for six hours straight. In the end Luca had immobilized them by shooting them with drugged darts. Two less imperial guards to dodge had been his reasoning for this.

Rather than leave them out in the sun, the guards had been left in the comfort of one of the villas. No dying of heat exhaustion for them with the effects of the drug set to wear off in around twelve hours.

What follows is two days of forced marches, of seeing imperial guards and following them to no end. It's something that soon has the vampires grumbling to the point Frankie has had enough. It's not her fault they're insisting on staying in their leather power rangers outfits.

"Fine, if you lot want to go home. Go home! But I'm staying. I can't leave people locked up for nothing more for than being clever or powerful.

How would you like it if it was your family stuck in there?" She spears each of them in turn, waiting until their gaze drops before carrying on. "So, are you staying or are you going, because I can have you on your way in seconds."

None of them takes her up on her offer. "Right in that case, no more whining for the love of all that's magical."

It's not until day four that they see William, again. That he's the spitting image of Zane comes as a shock to the rest of team. Dominik in particular looks to be having difficulty accepting this.

He looks back and forth between the Wereall and the Nautilus himself. "And here I was thinking one of you was bad enough." His voice is laced with enough disgust that Frankie has to stifle her laughter.

It's tempting to concentrate on Dex and have the Wereall commander as the Jack Russell's doppelganger. However, Frankie daren't while the man is awake. No, the less he knows of their presence, the better. It might be that they'll have better luck following him than his minions. While the imperial guard might be stuck at *Garnet Cove*, Frankie doubts William puts such limitations on himself.

He walks down to the beach, with the team

on his trail. That William is alone is interesting. Could it be he doesn't want his guards knowing where he's off to? Frankie suspects this is a big fat YES.

Sure enough on reaching the pristine white beach, William looks around sneakily before jumping down onto the sand. He then scuttles across it, making directly for one of the drinks cabanas that dot the beach.

Even though she knows it's not the Nautilus, it's bizarre watching what looks to be 'Zane' behaving this way. She can't imagine how the merman feels about it. Her ruminations are interrupted when she spots what William is up to. "No way! Please don't tell me all he's doing is grabbing a cocktail?"

"I sure hope you're wrong, Shortcake."

Instead of following the Wereall commander onto the hot sand, the group walks along the front of the resort. They can see him clearly from here without exposing themselves to excessive heat.

Frankie's mouth drops open when William stops next to the cabana. His furtive glances around before he darts inside speak volumes. He's definitely up to more than simply grabbing a drink.

They wait.

And then they wait some more. They even move into the shade cast by one of the beachfront villas. Unless he's whipping up Pina Coladas for his whole team, there's no way he should have taken this long.

"Jinxed jackrabbits, there's gotta be a portal inside the hut." Frankie lurches forward, and jumps down onto the beach. Only Zane pouncing on her and pushing her down into the hot sand stops her.

10

Frankie rolls onto her side, taking Zane with her. She can't roll any further. A backpack crammed full of explosives putting paid to this. "What the heck are you doing," she hisses out.

"I know you're keen to move ahead. But you can't race in half-cocked. We don't have a clue what we'll find. Also we need to sort out those two." His breath tickles her lips, so close is his mouth to hers.

Frankie pulls away from the gravitational pull of those luscious lips and looks around wildly. She's expecting to see a couple of the imperial guard bearing down on them. She can't see anyone. "Who are you talking about?"

Zane nods down the beach as though this will make things clear. It's not until Frankie struggles into a sitting position that she can see what he's talking about.

There are two people further along the beach

and they sure as Hades aren't sunbathing. The large stakes, even visible at this distance, are a testament to this.

"More of the island's security team?"

"Most likely."

Zane stands and helps her to her feet. "But where did they come from? There's no way they were on the island three days ago." Even though Frankie's ability to sense energy is new to her, there's no way she'd have missed them.

Zane doesn't bother answering her. Instead he transports himself down the beach magically. Apparently not willing to be left behind, the three vampires follow in his stead. They move fast enough that there's a whooshing sound as they displace the air. This along with a rooster tail of fine sand means that despite being invisible they're anything but convert.

Even from this distance it's easy to see Luca and Dominik wrenching the stakes out of the beach. They throw them far out into the bay reinforcing how loath they are to touch pointy bits of wood.

A moment later Zane waves his hand in the air. Frankie is returning the greeting when she realizes he's waving his wand. She yanks her hand back down by her side and examines her feet, hoping he hasn't seen her. As well as this, she shuts her brain down, keeping her embarrassment to herself.

"Zane must have sent the bodies back to their loved ones." Sophie follows this up by holding the front of her top out and blowing down her cleavage. It's gotta be hot having a hamster stuffed down there.

On looking up, Frankie can see the sand next to Zane and the vampires is once again pristine. Another wave of his wand and Zane, Luca and Magda return. Frankie rolls her eyes at the Nautilus leaving Dominik to find his own way back.

Zane opens his mouth to speak, but Frankie forestalls his words by holding up her hand. Only when Dominik returns does she fire her questions at Zane. It's something that has him stepping back and holding his own hands up.

"Whoa, whoa, whoa. Hold your seahorses, Shortcake."

Frankie clenches her fists by her side. She's not good with patience, especially not after four days of failure. She waits a beat before asking her most pressing question. "How long had they been dead?"

Zane slides his wand back into a slot on the side of his shorts, taking his own sweet time about it. "They weren't."

Frankie's eyes widen. "What? Then why did you get rid of them? We could have asked who pegged them out to dry."

Zane doesn't answer. Instead the three vamps shake their heads slowly, and in unison. "What?"

Frankie doesn't bother prettying her question up, there's no need.

It's Magda who answers. "Alive yes, but close to crossing over."

Luca finishes her sentence, something that's becoming more and more frequent. "And they needed medical attention, urgently."

Great, now Frankie feels like a right heel, more interested in information than the well-being of the security guys. Sure they've proved injurious to her and her friends in the past, but only when following orders. Knowing the Garnets to disobey a direct order would mean losing your job. Frankie imagines jobs of any kind are in short supply in this neighborhood.

Zane puts his hand on her shoulder to ease her guilt. "I sent them to the hospital at Nassau. The doctors won't know where they've come from, but should be able to help them."

Frankie's shoulders droop. "Hexed hobbits, we were this close to finding out who was responsible. If we could just have asked them who it was." She isn't sure how answers would help, but anything's better than being in the dark.

"We did ask, but they were delirious so it was pretty hard to get a straight answer," says Zane.

Magda chimes in to support this. "They ramble like drunk men. They know not who did this to them."

As incoherent as the two security guys had

been, it's still possible to piece together them being suckered by the whole Mad Hatters' Tea Party.

"But that makes no sense. Even if Aunt Betty drugged them by mistake why would she peg them out like that?" It doesn't matter how Frankie looks at it, there's no way to tie this in with a shotgun wedding. "We'll have to work on it when we get back from the *All Hallows Keep*." That's if they can find a way through to the fortress.

Nothing holding them back, the group moves onto the beach, pulling up behind the cabana. No matter how hard they listen there isn't any sound coming from inside.

"Nana Peg, do you want to take a peek? If he's there, just say you're looking for a way home."

Getting a nod of approval to this course of action, Frankie takes her wand and waves it around her Wereall relation. This has the woman once again visible, audible, and even sniffable to those outside the group. It also has the group no longer visible to Frankie's nana.

Frankie gives her Nana Peg the go-ahead by placing her hand in the middle of the woman's back and urging her forward. Nana Peg scoots around the end of the small hut. She stops, looking into the cabana in confusion. She then crooks her finger and the others join her. Frankie is soon as confused. "Now where's he gone?"

There no longer being a need for Nana Peg to

be visible, Frankie soon has her back in the safety of the group ward. If they're going to be walking into who knew what, then the fewer warnings, the better.

The cabana is empty but for half a dozen spirit bottles, a few limp fruit slices and some faded cocktail umbrellas. "It's gotta be a portal."

This much is obvious with none of them taking their eyes off the cabana for more than a second. And even if William had left the way he arrived, they'd still have spotted him scuttling back across the beach.

Frankie inches past Nana Peg and into the narrow space, scanning the walls, benches and cupboards for runic engravings. "Question is how does it open?"

She has to assume the portal can be operated in the same way as the one at the cliff face. There it's a case of find the runes, point her amulet at them and 'boom', they're in. Only there don't appear to be any runes. At least none she can see.

An even bigger question is what they'll face if they're lucky enough to open the portal? At the cliff face, they knew what was on the other side so far as the lay of the land. Here, they don't have a clue. They could open the portal and walk straight into a trap. It's been so easy to follow William here.

Perhaps too easy?

Frankie fans her face before looking to the

others. "We need to search every square inch of the cabana. He can't have just disappeared." She focuses her attention on Nana Peg. "He can't do that, can he?"

"No. No he can't."

Frankie thinks this is it when Nana Peg speaks again.

"Unless he's taken the power from someone who can, then, most definitely he could vanish."

"He can?" Frankie continues to peer at her nana, although her vision has turned inward. "Can you?"

"It is forbidden for those other than the anointed to take the powers of another."

Frankie isn't backing down. "But you can do it, right?"

Nana Peg's nod is hesitant. Even covered in fur as she is, Frankie can see the woman isn't happy about admitting to this ability. "So you could, for example, take a little from each of us?" Frankie waves a hand around encompassing the whole team.

Sophie and Stinky squeak loudly at this suggestion. Frankie can understand Sophie's reaction. The small witch isn't super powerful other than in the 'boom' and nursing departments. As to why the hamster is upset that's a mystery. Surely the small rodent doesn't have magical abilities?

Zane's quick to put Sophie, and even Stinky,

at their ease. "It would have to be those who had powers to spare."

Dex stops his examination of the floor of the cabana long enough to chip in. *"I'd give her some of my sniffing super powers, but she's already got her own."*

"We 'ave abilities we can spare," says Magda, with Luca and Dominik nodding in agreement.

On spotting the hackles on Nana Peg's neck standing to attention, Frankie holds her hand up. "What is it?"

"I... I... I can't. There are rules."

"Hah, rules! Like William hasn't broken a few by taking in prisoners so they can have their powers stolen from them by a demon. And let's not forget the pay-per-stay thing he's got going with the Garnet family."

"The penalties are severe."

"They can't be that bad, can they?" Sophie voices the question, Frankie had been about to.

Nana Peg nods mutely. On seeing everyone staring at her expectantly she whispers a single word. "Death!"

Frankie hadn't seen this coming. William really is a jerk. It takes a lot of persuasion to get Nana Peg to spit out the details. Apparently there used to be a time when all Wereall were allowed to take powers. Take them from those who'd broken the law, or were simply evil to the core.

This had all changed when William took over

after Peggy's father, Thalgos the Great, died. It had just taken two executions for the new rule to sink in with the populace.

Since then no Wereall had siphoned powers from a magical being. Not one. Frankie wasn't about to break a winning streak like this. "Okay, so no siphoning."

Nana Peg's relief is a palpable thing, her hackles settle back down, and her breathing evens out. No longer is she panting like a pooch that's been left in a hot car.

"Probably best you keep quiet about what you've been up to in the siphoning department, Shortcake."

Frankie wipes her brow of sweat before replying. *"Yeah, I was thinking the same thing."* She's not exactly in William's good books as it is.

"No point us dying of heat exhaustion, is there." Sophie waves her wand around the small cabana before pointing at each corner of the building. She hasn't had time to shove her wand back down the front of her bra, next to Stinky, when the air around them cools.

Frankie smiles broadly. "Thanks Sophie, my brain was starting to boil."

"Ewww boiled brains. Still, they'd be better than budget dog chow."

"Hah, like you've eaten any dog chow in living memory. It's a wonder you don't look like a muffin."

"Right!" Zane rubs his hands together in a business-like manner. "Stinky, you take ground level. Dex you're up from her. Frankie you check out the bar. I'll take the ceiling."

Obvious they're superfluous to requirements; Sophie, Nana Peg and the three vampires sit outside on the bamboo stools next to the bar top. For a moment Frankie is tempted to mix them something tropical. Not that this distracts her from searching her 'level' inch-by-inch.

Nothing, there's not a blasted rune in sight. There are however, lots of engravings that appear to be courtesy of the local indigenous people. Frankie even has a shot at holding her amulet and pointing it in their direction. Just in case.

Nope, not a bloomin' thing happens. "There has to be a way in, unless…"

Zane drops his gaze from the ceiling of the small hut. "Unless what?"

"What if it's not a portal? What if it's simply a secret passage? Dex, can you have a good sniff around the floor and see if you pick anything up?"

"Sure thing, Mom. I'm on it."

There follows a lot of sniffing and sneezing, with the floor of the hut being the beach itself. Frankie's watching Dex as he zigzags his way around the space, careful not to miss a spot. "Hang on Dex."

"What? Why? I'm not finished yet."

"There can't be a secret tunnel. Not with the sand as groomed as it is." It's while staring at the ground, something else makes itself plan to Frankie. Despite the four of them tramping around in there, the sand looks exactly as it had before they'd entered. "How can that be?"

"How can what be?" says Zane, staring at the ground with her.

"No footprints. Not one." Heck there aren't even any little hamster prints in evidence.

Zane hunkers down and grabs a handful of the pure white crystals that make up the beach. He pours them back down and they all watch as the sand goes back to exactly where it was before.

Nana Peg, who's leaning over the bar watching proceedings, sniffs loudly in disgust. "William must have taken the powers of someone very strong for this."

"Not really," say Sophie and Zane in unison.

It's Zane who continues. "It looks to be a fairly basic 'clean your room' spell."

"A what!?" Frankie stares aghast at her fellow coven members. "You mean I've been dealing with drifts of dog hair all this time for nothing."

Zane shrugs. Sophie meantime covers her mouth with her hand.

Dex is not amused. *"I'm not THAT bad."*

Frankie spears her familiar with a gaze that tells him, he's fooling no-one. *"There are dust bunnies in our cabin that are positively feral."*

Frankie kicks the sand and watches in fascination as every last grain returns to where it had been before.

"As soon as we're back aboard the *Pearl*, I need that spell."

A secret passage back on the cards, Frankie and the others proceed to pull, shove and push anything and everything. Frankie even moves the bottles of alcohol and the container of small umbrellas. Just because it looks innocuous, doesn't make it so.

It's on moving a bowl of dried up lime cheeks that something finally happens. The ground gives way under them, plunging her, Zane and the two familiars into the darkness below.

11

The four of them land in a heap under the trapdoor, with it slamming shut before Frankie has time to call out to the others. Even with this brief window of light, Frankie knows they're not alone.

She isn't concerned about the man in the room attacking them. He's way past caring. This is the fourth body so far, putting them way above what she's been expecting by around, well four.

"Mom, are we okay? Please tell me we're okay, because this place doesn't smell okay."

"Were okay, Dex. The man can't hurt us."

Frankie's answered him before pondering the question to any great degree. Better not to have the small dog bouncing off the walls in an effort to escape. It's then she hears squeaking from behind her. "Stinky, are you alright?"

Manic squeaking is followed by an equally squeaky "No".

"Okay, it's time to play find the hamster."

"That's not something I ever thought I'd hear you say," says Zane, spluttering with laughter.

Frankie ignores him, instead groping around in the dark in search of Sophie's familiar. She can hear the Nautilus is doing likewise even if he's giving into the occasional chortle. Frankie's finally rewarded when she grabs a handful of wiry fur. "You're safe now."

Frankie stuffs the small rodent down the front of her top, Sophie-style. Immediately the small animal relaxes. It's something Frankie is able to detect by its heartbeat slowing. Eventually it turns around and pokes its head out of her top. Shame there's nothing for it to see.

Frankie holds her wand over her head and says "Illuminate!" like she really means it. Nothing happens. "Blast, it looks as this is another no-go area on the magic front."

Thank goodness experience has them all packing headlamps. They haven't had time to get these from their backpacks when the trapdoor opens again. This time it doesn't close, with a sun lounger being jammed in the gap to stop this from happening.

The first person Frankie sees peering through the opening is a grinning Dominik. "Can anyone join the party?"

He really does think this is a boy's own adventure. Sure Frankie likes a bit of mayhem as much as the next witch. However, Dominik's glee is at a whole different level. He jumps into the space, landing softly on his feet and close enough to Frankie that she knows it's been no accident. He's soon joined by the others, with Sophie transporting herself and Nana Peg into the space magically.

This has Frankie realizing that with the trapdoor open she might be able to perform magic down here after all. Unlike the Wereall caving system where all magical powers are suspended, the same doesn't appear to be true in this space. At least so long as the trapdoor is open.

The first thing she needs to do is get rid of the body. Already the heat and the humidity of the island are seeping into the space, warming it up.

A glimpse before she sends him on his way shows he was a bartender at the resort. The badge on his tropical shirt proclaiming that in life he'd answered to Manuel, Mixologist. She sends him back to his family as Zane had done with the first lot of guards they'd found.

It's when Zane mutters an incantation under his breath and holds his wand aloft, that the true horror of Manuel's passing becomes visible. There are scratches all over the walls, showing the bartender hadn't gone quietly. It's enough to have Frankie swallowing deeply. Dex likewise has gone quiet, something that's unusual for him.

He's not even humming telepathically as is his habit.

Frankie gives into a shudder. It does nothing to shake free the remaining horror factor. "Okay, there has to be another way out of here. Let's find it." Rather than keep searching by the light of their wands, the team is soon sporting headlamps. Much safer if their hands are free for smacking people than stuck holding a torch. Even Dex is wearing a specially adapted headlamp that has him looking like a small furry potholer.

Zane swings around, taking in the entire group. The beam from his headlamp bounces around the room, blinding all of them. Even Stinky doesn't escape from her spot back down Sophie's top.

"Careful," says Frankie holding her hand up in front of her eyes. "You'll muck up our night vision if you keep that up."

Zane immediately looks at the floor. "Sorry, what I wanted to say was let's examine every inch of every surface. Push every rock, move every pebble."

It's a good reminder from the Nautilus. If simply moving a bowl of lime cheeks can gain access to the chamber, it should be as simple to leave again. At least Frankie hopes so. If they're to continue following William, they need to leave and not back the way they've just come.

Frankie points her headlamp up at the ceiling before looking around the group as Zane has just done. "If anyone finds any runes, no matter how small, let me know. Okay?" She gets nods in response from the whole team, the beams of light flying around the space giving it a nightclub air.

Five minutes of searching and Frankie's starting to believe it's a bust. Then Dex calls out telepathically.

"Mom, I've found something!"

His head being jammed in the corner where Manuel had breathed his last has her gulping. Just what on earth is it that the Jack Russell has discovered? Knowing Dex, it could just as easily be a discarded candy bar wrapper, or a forgotten sandwich, and not a way out.

"Whatcha found, buddy?" Frankie gets down on her hands and knees next to him, careful to avoid any damp patches on the ground. Sure enough on illuminating the area with her headlamp, she spots a dried crust. "Sheesh Dex, do you ever not think about food?"

"What? Not that. Left a bit."

Frankie looks to the left as he's instructed. Bingo! The runes are small and if Dex hadn't been on patrol, she doubts anyone else in the team would have spotted them. "Okay, we've got something." Her words echo around the chamber. Rather than stay right next to the runes on her hands and knees, she stands again. "Dex, by my side."

Only when the team is well away from the corner where the runes are located, does Frankie take hold of her amulet. Experience says when these portals open it can be fairly spectacular. She's expecting the same here. "Okay, are we all ready?" Again there's a nightclub's worth of flashing lights in return.

On looking around the group, Frankie's reminded that only the three vampires are dressed for battle. It's something she rectifies with a wave of her wand, taking care of herself, Nana Peg and Dex.

Like the vampires, Frankie also opts for leather. It'll help protect them from the cold as well as any claws they might encounter. Not that she lumbers them all with onesies. No, she goes for hard-wearing clothing topped off with full-length leather coats. Practical, yet stylish. She also reinstates Dex and her nana's fur ensuring they won't risk hypothermia.

They're all ready for Frankie to open the portal. Zane and Sophie stand with their wands out in front of them while the three vampires appear surprisingly relaxed. Only Nana Peg looks nervous about what they'll face. It's for this reason Frankie puts her hands on the woman's shoulders and gently edges her backward. No point having the weakest link out front and centre.

"Right, here we go." Frankie angles her amulet down at the runes. For a second nothing happens, and then all hell breaks loose. The entire rock wall swings open in their direction. It does so with enough force that if any of them had been in the way, they'd have been squished like bugs. Thank goodness Frankie had sent Manuel's body back to his family. There would have been no recognizing him after that dramatic opening.

Zane whistles through his teeth. "Phew, that's a nasty little extra if you don't have your wits about you."

He's about to step into the space beyond when Frankie stops him. "Hang on a second. I need to hit us with a concealment spell."

Sophie's brow wrinkles before she puts her question into words. "But we're already covered by Zane's spell. Surely we don't need another."

It's Zane who answers on Frankie's behave. "If we want the spell to stay in place, Frankie's the one who needs to cast it. My magic doesn't stick once we cross into the realm of the Wereall."

No more questions in the offing, Frankie takes care of a spell that should be identical to that already cast by Zane. And that's with the emphasis on the 'should be'. She hopes they remain invisible, inaudible and whatever the sniff equivalent is of that line-up. The one way she'll know if she's been successful is when they arrive at *All Hallows Keep*.

The spell in place, Zane wastes no time in marching out of the stone cell. Dominik is hot on his heels, determined not to be left out of any potential chaos. This has Frankie moving forward too, adrenalin already pumping through her system in readiness. She's flanked by Luca and Magda, with the weaker members of the crew coming up the rear.

"What the heck?" Frankie's having trouble coming to terms with the space they've entered. The most eye-catching thing about the room is the view beyond the floor to ceiling windows. If she's not mistaken, it's Central Park and they're high up enough that this has to be a penthouse.

The furnishings are sleek and modern and nothing like those at *All Hallows Keep*. She walks into the open area, spotting a top of the line kitchen off to one side. Out on the patio area is a Jacuzzi that could easily seat ten. "It would appear William doesn't like roughing it with the prisoners."

"When I find him, I will kill him for this." Frankie swings around to face Nana Peg, and words fail her. Gone is the animal form, instead a stunning older woman stands before her. Something else that's gone is the woman's timid nature with her looking more than capable of murder. Huh, there's a surprise.

Unfortunately due to her change in shape, Peggy's leather coat hangs loosely from her shoulders. The most surprising thing is that her nana's hair is a brilliant silver, setting her olive skin off to perfection. Her eyes, however, remain as green as always, and a fair match for the color of Frankie's own.

When Frankie had first heard the lethal words from Nana Peg, she'd thought them an empty threat. "What's got you so riled?"

"These, these do not belong to my sister."

It takes a second for Frankie to focus on what it is her relation is holding up. Perhaps it's that the panties have more in common with dental floss than lingerie. Either way, Frankie's confused.

"What's your sister got to do with this?"

Nana Peg drops the offending garment back on the end of the black, leather sofa before she answers. "Selena, my sister, and your great aunt, is married to William. She does not know of... of..." Nana Peg waves her hand around the large space, "this lifestyle of his. She's stuck at the keep while he lives the high-life."

"Selena? She's the one who helped us when we were last there. I think you'll find she does know about this. She sure as heck knew about his dalliance with Mimi Merriweather."

"I'm going to make sure she knows exactly what he's been up to when we visit. For too long William has kept us apart too long."

Frankie adds another item to the list of outcomes from their visit to *All Hallows Keep*. 'Save

Aunt Selena from a life of hell' is near the top. While she's at it, Frankie mentally adds another great aunt to her growing family tree.

A quick glance over her shoulder shows it to be her and Nana Peg still in the great room. The others, including Dex, are off searching the place, looking for William. Or even another portal that will take them to the keep itself. The Jack Russell humming away tunelessly tells Frankie he hasn't run into anything dire.

"Oooh, steak."

The sound of a fridge door opening off to her right has Frankie marching in that direction. "What have I told you about eating anything you find? You have no idea if it's been laced with something."

Despite the large size of the penthouse, Frankie is next to Dex in front of the fridge a second or two later. Even as quick as she's been, all she can see of the small dog is his rear end. His tail wagging delightedly tells of him having found something tasty.

However, it's not this that catches her eye. It's the fridge magnets that pepper the door. Pithy sayings and pictures of scantily clad women make up the majority. However, there's one that has her dragging Dex out of fridge and slamming the door, hard. Certainly it's hard enough that a slew of near-naked women end up on the floor.

Frankie kicks them under the appliance before Dominik or Zane can see them.

In preparation, she takes a couple of steps back from the large double-door fridge. She has to force Dex to do the same, with his nose firmly jammed against the door seal. She's joined by Nana Peg. If the fridge is what Frankie thinks it is, the whole team needs to be in here, pronto.

"Everyone in the kitchen now!"

12

The team returns to the penthouse kitchen in ones and twos, each of them reporting they've seen no sign of William. All of them to a man, woman and hamster eyes Frankie's nana with suspicion.

"Don't be like that. It's Nana Peg." She gets a series of dropped jaws and wide eyes in response to this revelation, although the team accepts it otherwise.

Dominik helps himself to an apple from the bowl on the counter. "Looking good, Peggy." He takes a big crunchy bite and speaks around it. "The place is like a show home." Juice sprays out along with his words forcing Frankie to step back.

The others support his summation.

"It's as if he uses the place for 'entertainment' only," says Zane, with a grimace.

This coupled with the G-string on the back of

the sofa, says William is most definitely not being faithful to Frankie's Aunt Selena. Now she's as angry as Nana Peg had been, when holding up the offending scrap of lace.

There being no point in them staying any longer, Frankie takes out her wand and holds it at the ready. "Okay, if this leads where I think it does, we need to be prepared for anything."

Frankie stands in front of the large fridge, her wand in one hand her amulet in the other. She's itching, literally, to free those prisoners that have no right being locked up.

Frankie sure hopes Nana Peg is right about her being able to detect evil. And tough if William's decree says this is a no-no. Probably to stop anyone from picking up he's evil enough to be an inmate and not the warden. It hadn't taken much to persuade Nana Peg in her human form to agree to use this inherent trait. Compared to her totem, the human Peggy is a bad ass.

Frankie's relieved that Peggy is willing to help, even if this involves breaking the law. The thought of accidentally unleashing another Mimi Merriweather on the world isn't to be borne. It's bad enough the she-devil's residual power lurks inside Frankie.

The team as ready as they'll ever be, Frankie points her amulet at what looks like a fridge magnet. The whole appliance shimmers for a second or two before the doors fly open. This proves beyond doubt the little hunk of plastic is nowhere near as mundane as the surrounding magnets.

Zane is first through the gap although he has to fight Dominik for the privilege. Frankie shakes her head at the pair of them before following in their stead. Next come Dex, Nana Peg and Sophie with a bra full of hamster. Last are Luca and Magda, joined at the hip as always.

Frankie is pleased she's still wearing her headlamp. Pointing it toward the ceiling, she turns it on illuminating the small space. She recognises the storage cupboard they've arrived in. She's been in here before.

It's also interesting that this particular portal should take them in through the mess hall located next to the *Syphonia*. It's this device that strips inmates of any magical abilities before they're transferred to the keep itself.

It would make more sense in Frankie's mind that William's penthouse was linked to his quarters in the tower at the keep. At least then he wouldn't need to traipse the length of the small island to go to bed. Her puzzlement must show on her face because Nana Peg comments on it.

"Hmmmph, trust my odious brother-in-law to keep the entry to his love nest well away from my sister."

Zane puts his finger to his lips, signalling

everyone to be quiet so he can hear what's happening on the other side of the door. He pulls his head away from it, frowning. "I can't hear anything, but that's not to say there isn't anyone on the other side."

Being able to hear what's happening in the room beyond isn't the only way of finding out if it's occupied. Frankie knows there's another way. "Dex, can you have a good sniff under the door?" It was the small dog smelling sausages that led them to this entry last time they were here. Surely the aroma of food would indicate the room is in use.

His sniffing is loud in the confined space; his telepathic response is also loud.

"Nothing! I can't even pick up day-old toast."

Frankie has to smile. His reply is heavy with disappointment. "Dex can't pick anything up. The room has to be empty."

"Perhaps I should enter first," says Nana Peg. "They're used to seeing me at the keep from time-to-time, although perhaps not coming in this way."

Frankie touches her nana's arm. "Stand tall, act like you're meant to be there, and no-one will say a thing." This has definitely worked for Frankie in the past.

"Hang on a second. Peggy won't be visible to anyone unless you can lift the concealment spell."

Frankie mentally smacks herself. It's so easy to forget they're all invisible to others when she can see everyone in the team as clear as day. Question is will her magic work in here? For sure it doesn't work when she's out in the caving system. Only when she's traversed this magical no-man's-land and is on the island proper do her powers return.

There's one way to find out. Frankie rummages around in her pockets, eventually locating her wand. She mutters a reversal under her breath and then taps Nana Peg on the shoulder. Outwardly there's no change. The one way they'll know if it's worked is if there's anyone in the mess hall.

"While I admire your confidence, child, you do realize your powers don't work in here." Nana Peg then smiles in an effort to alleviate the sting of her words.

Frankie smiles broadly. "You wanna bet?" She then points her wand at a gigantic tin of baked beans on the shelf next to her. A second later the tin levitates. "Okay, we're good to go."

"That can't be possible. Even with your Wereall blood you shouldn't be able to access your powers in here."

Frankie shrugs nonchalantly. "Are you ready, Nana?" She's looking to see if the older woman is going to cope with any potential conflict. Instead of any sign of nerves, she gets a business-like nod in response. Frankie could get to like this new and feistier Peggy.

Her nana already has a hold of the door handle when Dex pipes up.

"Why don't we go out the back way?

"Hang on a second," says Frankie, given she's the one who's heard him. It's enough to have Nana Peg releasing the handle.

Without explaining the hold up, Frankie spins on the spot. She's been hoping to examine the back wall of the storage cupboard. Instead she finds herself hard up against Dominik's chest. It's something that has him smiling broadly. She can't help but smile in return. His humor is infectious, like small pox.

It's something that has Zane trying to squeeze through to her side. No way does Frankie want the pair coming to blows in such a confined space. She keeps her smile in place and then points her wand casually at Dominik's face. "Outta my way or I'll remove your teeth."

Now it's Dominik who's desperately squeezing into a different spot. Fortunately he's moved enough to give her a good view of the back wall. Frankie angles her headlamp down and examines the space, pushing canned goods to the side as necessary. "Found 'em." Sure enough right there at eye-level is a set of runes.

"No point going out the front way, when we can sneak out the back." Frankie holds her amulet up and the now-familiar beam of light shoots out and latches onto the runes. The whole wall slides to one side. "What? Are you kidding me?" Instead of exiting onto the barren lump of rock that houses *All Hallows Keep* they're looking at a bedroom. A circular bed, black satin sheets, and a mirrored ceiling point to this being in the penthouse. It's something that's confirmed by Sophie.

"Perhaps try the amulet up the other way?" suggests Nana Peg.

Frankie's never needed to use the runes on the back of her amulet. Now's as good an opportunity as any to give them a whirl. She briefly points it back at the runes and is pleased to see the wall slide shut again. She then flips her it over and repeats the process.

This time the wall swings away from them rather than sliding to the side. Frankie knows immediately that the runes on the reverse of her amulet have worked a charm. "That's better."

Instead of facing yet another grossly over-decorated room in William's penthouse, they're looking out onto barren rock. Frankie knows exactly where they are even if the landscape is anything but welcoming.

Everyone safely out of the storage cupboard and the large rock restored, Frankie checks they're all ready. The last thing she does is add Nana Peg back into her camouflage ward.

Finally, they're back on track and following the revised plan they'd sweated over at the restaurant. If she closes her eyes, Frankie can see the whiteboard as clearly as if it was right in front of her.

"Okay, William you jerk, coming ready or not."

Not until they move around the pile of rocks they're standing behind do Sophie, Luca and Dominik see the keep for the first time. The trio gasps in unison, and Frankie isn't far behind. Zane indulges in a couple of words that tell he's not impressed either. Even Magda is muttering under her breath, half in English and half in her mother-tongue. It's not seeing the keep again that's got Frankie, Zane and Magda riled; it's that the place has doubled in size. Oh and let's not forget the addition of machine-gun posts around the top perimeter. It would appear William is expecting company.

Frankie stands with hands on hips and stares at the formidable structure. "How on earth did he know we were coming? We were so careful on the island. Unless…"

"Unless what, Shortcake?"

"Unless it's not us he's expecting? It could be the person who took out the island's security guards."

Magda turns to Frankie, without leaving the

shelter of Luca's arms. "You mean your Aunt Betty?"

"Could be, although I'm still not one hundred percent certain Calico Jack is telling the truth about that. He thinks nothing of lying if it will further his aims." There's something off about her granddad's assertions that her mysterious aunt is after an official union. Something Frankie can't put her finger on.

Silence falls on the group as they make their way along the very edge of the island. Even though they're invisible, it's best not to run into any of the guards who patrol the glorified chunk of rock. That the guards keep well back from the edges is likely down to the sharks that circle the island. Even Frankie isn't keen on getting too close. She doesn't like swimming at the best of times, never mind when the water is a dark slate gray and infested with things that bite.

As with their last visit to the keep, the group pulls up at the back of the humongous castle-like structure. For whatever reason, the guards don't walk around here. Frankie thinks it might be down to there being no freaking doors or windows. It wasn't something that stopped Frankie and her friends from gaining entrance last time they were here.

Frankie's got her wand out and has even levitated everyone a foot off the ground, when Nana Peg cries out. The terror on the woman's face has

Frankie settling them back down again. "You didn't say anything at the café about being afraid of heights." Frankie's unable to keep the annoyance out of her voice. She doesn't even try. It's something that shows on Nana Peg's face, her expression morphing from apologetic to angry in a heartbeat.

The stately woman appears to have quite the fight to get control of her rage. Only then does she speak. "My intention was always to go directly to my sister by another way."

Frankie steps closer to her nana, getting all up in her face. "And you were going to share this with us when?"

"Calm down. It makes no odds if Peggy enters the keep by another way."

Frankie jerks her shoulder displacing Zane's hand and then turns on him. It's something that has him backing off in surrender.

Dominik, however, whistles through his teeth and mutters, "Feisty. I like feisty."

This has her turning on him next, she's so angry she's in danger of putting her wand through his heart. Shame her new wand isn't made of wood.

"Mom, are you okay? You smell funny?"

Frankie glares at Dex and is immediately contrite. His tail between his legs he rolls onto his back and bares his tummy. Dex is never submissive, even when she threatens him with the vet. "Oh buddy, I'm sorry. I'm not mad at you." Frankie hunkers down and after rubbing his tummy, rolls the shivering dog right side up. *"What do you mean I smell funny?"* While she has some idea, it's always good to get a second opinion, even if it is canine in nature.

"You stink like that lady you had the big fight with last time we were here."

"You mean Mimi Merriweather?"

"I dunno. Probably."

Even though Dex can't remember the name of the Succubus, Frankie having mentioned the woman's name has Zane peering at her. "Why are you talking about that she-devil?"

Blast, Frankie had been so wound up she didn't even realize that part of the conversation with Dex had been audible. "Dex says I smell like her."

"That could explain your, ah…"

Zane doesn't say anything further. There really isn't a need. Frankie knows exactly what he means. As she's just done with Dex, Frankie next apologizes to her nana and then Zane. At least with them she doesn't need to rub their tummies although she wouldn't say no with Zane. She doubts he'd say no either.

"You can rub my tummy any time, Shortcake."
"OMG, I can still hear you inside my head."

Zane looks at her, a bemused expression on

his face. *"This is interesting. We're getting closer all the time."*

As tempting as it is to move closer as Zane has suggested, Frankie has her eye on the prize, and this time, it's not the gorgeous Nautilus.

13

Once again Frankie looks up at the granite wall towering over them. If not this way, how was Nana Peg hoping to get inside the keep without being seen?

"Nana Peg, this other way in, where is it exactly?"

Now it's her Wereall relation's turn to give one of those multi-purpose European shrugs. Okay, so no freaking idea. Frankie has to fight to keep her anger under control. What is it about being back at *All Hallows Keep* that has her inner demon clamoring for release?

Might it be that there are demons in the keep whose energy she's picking up on? It wouldn't surprise her. *The Lore of Crafte,* the Marina Coven's grimoire, says demons are generally not nice. Talk about understatement.

"I say we search for another way in," says Sophie, her head angled back as she stares at the cliff of granite in front of them. "I hadn't realized the wall would be quite this high."

Truth be told, neither had Frankie. Does this mean there are even more inmates now? Or is this all down to defending the keep against any and all comers? Frankie hopes it's the latter. As it is, they'll have their hands full processing the five hundred odd prisoners that had been here before.

"I have heard tell of a way in around here." Nana Peg falls silent, not that she's inactive. Instead she's scanning the wall to her left and then her right. She then moves along the wall and repeats the process.

Frankie catches on at the same time as everyone else, with the team spreading out. How feverishly they search the granite wall for any sign of runes tells Frankie how loath they are to go over the top. It's a squeak from Stinky that confirms the hamster has hit pay dirt. Sure enough, right down next to the ground is a small set of runes. Unsure what's going to happen, everyone moves well clear. For all they know a huge slab of granite could swing out and flatten the lot of them.

It doesn't. What happens is far more spectacular.

A large block of granite slams out of the wall by around five feet, cantilevered in place. Another follows, and then another, continuing on up to the top of the keep. While it might not have a balustrade, it's definitely a staircase.

Zane already has his foot on the first step before he announces, "I'll go first."

He's taken Dominik by surprise and once again the hunky vampire has to follow in the merman's footsteps. Frankie goes next, followed by Dex, Nana Peg, Sophie and Stinky in a C cup. Magda and Luca bring up the rear. All of them without exception stare at the wall as they stomp up the stairs. Better this than looking at the sheer drop off on the other side.

On hearing Luca hissing, "Hurry, hurry," Frankie risks a quick peak back down the staircase. She's expecting to see Wereall guards swarming after them. What she sees is far more alarming. The steps are disappearing back into the wall behind Magda's husband. And they're gaining on him.

Frankie turns back around and sprints to catch up with Dominik. She then pushes on his back urging him and therefore Zane to greater speed. She knows the rest of the team is right behind her. The threat of falling to your death will do that to you.

As they explode onto the top of the keep, Frankie wastes no time in finding her wand. She flicks the guards who are manning the nearest machine guns far out into the sea. She isn't completely heartless, surrounding them with a protection spell that also blocks their screams. This way they won't be heard by William and also won't end up as a shark's chew toy. It's win/win so far as Frankie's concerned.

Unfortunately their absence doesn't go unnoticed. Even if the guards can't see Frankie and the other team members, they know something is up. Their comrades suddenly missing in action speaks loudly of this.

Frankie jerks her head briefly at the other guards who are swarming in their direction. "Zane, Dominik can you take care of that lot?" She doesn't wait for confirmation before turning back toward the stairs. It's going to be a close-run thing, with the stairs disappearing as Luca lifts each foot.

It's not a risk she's prepared to take, so to heck with them not being keen on heights. Frankie points her wand at the trailing members of the group and levitates them up and onto the top of the keep. It's not a moment too soon with the staircase slamming back into the wall immediately after.

Dex is shaking like he's wet, and the others aren't looking too hot, either. "You're all safe now." Frankie tries for reassuring. It doesn't appear to be working. Perhaps this is because they're all looking over her shoulder rather than at her.

Sure enough on turning she finds Zane and

Dominik grappling with half a dozen guards apiece. Talk about a couple of dog piles. The element of surprise no longer with them, Frankie doesn't hesitate. A casual wave of her wand and the guards fly overhead, their destination wet and cold.

Zane gets slowly to his feet before reluctantly bending over and offering Dominik his hand. The vampire just as reluctantly takes it. "I don't understand. I should be able to take on that many guards with ease."

Luca looks to be as confused. "And I should have been able to run up those stairs carrying those slower than myself."

Frankie shakes her head slowly and even indulges in an eye roll. Sheesh what is it about men not listening. "Guys, we told you it was going to be this way. We warned you."

Dominik rubs the back of his neck. "Yeah, but I didn't think that would apply to vampires." Luca nods enthusiastically in support of this sentiment.

"I did explain to them about us losing our powers." Magda doesn't try to hide her annoyance. "They said it was different for the male vampire."

Again Frankie has to fight to keep her annoyance under wraps. "It applies to everyone who visits the keep."

"Except you, Shortcake."

Frankie's holds her hands out, palms up. What can she say, she's special. She also knows the roof of the keep is not what it appears to be. It's this that has her screaming at Dominik to stay where he is, that it's dangerous. He turns, gives her a cocky grin and continues his exploration of the roof.

He disappears a second later and if not for Frankie's quick levitation spell, he'd have been splattered all over the floor of the courtyard. As it is, he's probably lost a few years, and possibly warned anyone below that they've got company. Even though the vampire is invisible, his plunging through the hologram has ripples spreading out in all directions.

Annoyed that he's possibly given the game away, Frankie takes pleasure in how white he is. His chalky complexion is pale even for a vampire. He's also seen what lies below. Unfortunately what's below might also have seen someone is up here. Someone other than the guards, that is, with them unlikely to tamper with the hologram as Dominik has done.

In unspoken agreement, the group closes up. The stronger members are at the front, the weaker at the back. Zane, Dominik and Luca position themselves, ready to take out any guards using their fighting skills. Frankie has her wand at the ready.

They wait.

Nothing happens.

They wait some more.

The holographic image stays in place.

No guards appear through it.

They've been lucky.

Very lucky.

Frankie shoves her wand back up her sleeve and turns to Dominik. She has to fold her arms to stop herself from throttling him. "You wanna tell us what you saw?"

Even having had time to get over it, his reply is staccato, shot at her in words and syllables. He really has been all shook up by the experience. None of it makes any sense. She suspects if he was speaking normally it would still be gibberish.

Frankie drops to her stomach and caterpillars along until she can feel the edge of the wall. She isn't too worried about guards descending on them now. If that was going to happen, it would have happened by now. She inches forward until she's able to bend forward from her waist. She's grateful for whoever it is who grabs her ankles. She suspects it's Zane.

After closing her eyes she leans forward, plunging her head through the illusion of solid granite. On risking a squint, she wants to slam her eyes shut again. She doesn't. If anything they might even open a little wider. No wonder Dominik had been at a loss for words. She is too.

The additional rows of cells are horrifying.

However, it's the tent-foot tall pile of wood in the middle of the open area that shocks her most. There isn't so much as a stray twig on the island, so how on earth has William rustled up this much wood? There's magic afoot here.

This pales compared to the real problem she faces. And that's Anne and Calico Jack being lashed to a pole atop this fire hazard. That William is standing next to it armed with a box of matches and an evil grin doesn't bode well for the pair. Interestingly the Wereall looks like he had when she'd first met him at *Magic Beans* all those months ago. This is a mash-up somewhere between Zane and Dominik. Hmmm, she hadn't even met Dominik back then. How had the Wereall known what would appeal to her on a subconscious level?

In his current guise, the Wereall leader stands just over six foot, with a physique that's similar to Zane's. However rather than dark brown hair, he's blond like Dominik. It's a deadly combination.

Her granddad unable to work his magic on this side of the veil means it's down to her to save them. Question is does she want to? They've been nothing but a pain in the proverbial since the day she met them.

It's something she's going to have to think on. She's learned the hard way about making snap decisions about these two.

Frankie isn't able to tell if William can actually see her, or if he's just guessing she's up there. Certainly the cloak of invisibility worked with the guards manning the machine guns. She reaches behind her and taps the top of the battlement. Sure enough Zane drags her backward until she's no longer hanging over the edge of the abyss.

Her mind back on using the machine guns to their advantage, her gaze settles on the one nearest to her. It's like something out of a technology museum, albeit in mint condition. No rust or cobwebs on this one. Mind you, the one Dex is giving some special attention might be in for some rust soon. Frankie's unable to squelch her smile in response to his, "This is now MINE!" expression.

She knows they can't fire the guns randomly into the open area in the middle of the keep. The chances of hitting Calico Jack and Anne would be too great. Then there are the prisoners whose cells face the open courtyard. She has no idea if the force fields that front these spaces can stop bullets. Fine if Frankie and the others take out some truly evil beings. What if they wing someone who's innocent?

Zane helps her to stand and then dusts her free of tiny stones.

His action has been perfunctory. This doesn't stop her heart fluttering in delight. It's something she stomps on immediately, needing to keep her head in the game. "I think he's expecting us. He's got Anne and Calico Jack and much as I'd like to leave them, I can't."

Zane's brows knot in confusion. "Why on earth not? They wouldn't think twice about ditching you."

"Yeah, and if I was tied to a big old stake with a heap of kindling at my feet, ya think they'd leave me then?" Frankie's interested in Zane's opinion on this, because she isn't one hundred percent sure herself.

Her description of Calico Jack and Anne's dilemma does however have the group on their bellies. Even Nana Peg is down there. This leaves Frankie and Dex on their own atop the battlements. Well, that is apart from the six seemingly headless bodies lying on the cold stone next to them. Stinky sits on the backs of Sophie's leg as if the added weight of one hamster will stop her witch from over-balancing.

Frankie crouches down next to the small pup, knowing his shaking is down to anticipation and not nerves. "You wanna check it out too?"

"Can I?" Still he doesn't move from his spot next to her feet.

"Sure, but let's find you a safer spot than this lot are using." As when they'd visited the keep last time, Frankie finds the edge of the parapet. She then moves carefully along it until she finds what it is she's after. However brief her scan of the courtyard has been, it's enough. She knows the location of the stairs used by the guards to get to their posts. It's here that it will be safe for Dex to see beyond the hologram without falling to his death.

It'll also allow her to scan the place without her back muscles cramping.

She and Dex, scramble down the stairs, both of them on their tummies to keep as low a profile as possible. Perhaps it's that Frankie's past is littered with failed spells that she's cautious. This might also account for Dex being in a similar position. No point in pushing their luck more than they already are.

Finally they settle, with Frankie sprawled over four steps. It's not the best, but it's easier than being suspended over a dizzying drop. Dex squeezes himself into the gap under her tummy. She welcomes his warmth seeping through the layers of clothing between them.

Frankie scans the courtyard, taking everything in. Of interest is that William hasn't moved from his previous spot. He's still standing there legs apart holding that box of matches.

What Frankie isn't expecting is him staring at the exact spot she and Dex are hiding, his gaze unwavering. This has her second guessing her concealment spell. She third guesses it when he theatrically slides the box open and retrieves a match.

14

Frankie holds her breath, ready to throw an extinguishing spell at William and that dreaded match. However, he doesn't do anything. Bejinxed badgers, is he faking it?

Surely if he knew she was up here, he'd light the match. Perhaps it's because he knows she can perform magic while at the keep? Even though she hadn't done so in front of him last time, he's bound to know she used magic then.

"Hah, he doesn't know we're here!" Dex's telepathic crowing is full of bravado. That is until he adds a tentative, *"Does he?"*

"I don't think so." Frankie's automatically answered him telepathically. She isn't sure why, but her gut has said this is the sensible thing to do. And has it ever let her down? No, it hasn't.

William seemingly frozen in place, Frankie moves her attention away from him. A quick scan of the floor of the keep and she moves onto the cells that surround it. In particular, she checks out the new layers, the granite used to build them not yet blackened with age.

Last time there had been five levels, housing an estimated one hundred prisoners per level. Now the headcount looks to be closer to a thousand. Of interest is the top layer looks more like a lingerie show than a house of correction. Could it be William has transported some of his 'friends' from the New York penthouse to here?

Frankie jerks her head in the direction of those who are doing time for being beautiful. This has Dex looking at them too.

"Whoa. Nana Peg's going nuts when she sees that lot."

Of more interest to Frankie is why Selena, William's wife hasn't done so already. Then Frankie spots her. At least she thinks it's her. This particular inmate stands out for a couple of reasons. Firstly, she's not dressed in scraps of lace. Secondly, her hair is gorgeous silver, with its color down to maturity and not three hours at the salon. Even though Frankie has never seen her aunt in human form, her resemblance to Nana Peg is uncanny.

"Now I'm mad. Him locking up his wife up so he can have his fancy ladies close at hand? That's evil!"

Nothing else of note to see, apart from how many guards there are, they retreat up the stairs.

They find Nana Peg straining against Zane and Dominik who are holding her down.

"Let me at him. I'll kill him with my bare hands."

Dex scoots behind Frankie to avoid being kicked by one of Nana Peg's thrashing legs. *"Yep, I was right. She's steaming mad."*

"Yeah, and she's going to be even angrier when she finds out William's locked up her sister." Frankie knows her nana won't yet be aware of this, with Selena's cell being right beneath their feet. Her nana will go ballistic when she finds out the true depth of William's depravity.

His keeping his bits of fluff on the premises is one thing. Locking up your wife so you can do so is another whole level of evil, in this case, the top level.

It takes a minute or two, but eventually Nana Peg settles down. Zane and Dominik even loosen their hold on her.

Frankie looks at each man in turn. "Zane, Dominik, I wouldn't be too hasty, if I was you." She then looks at her nana deciding the 'removing a plaster' method of breaking the news will be best. "Selena is locked up alongside the other women." Wow, usually it's 'other woman', as in singular. William really is an overachiever.

Sure enough as the news filters through to her nana, she goes from being reasonably relaxed to furious again. Dex comes close to getting his head kicked in. Enough is enough. Their plans have taken quite a battering. Nana Peg losing it like she is will have them in tatters.

Frankie grabs her wand from the sleeve of her coat and swirls it over the top of her writhing nana. Pink sparkles shoot out the end of the delicate stem of silver. These drift down, coating the woman from head to toe. Zane and Dominik also cop their fair share, not that it will do them any harm.

The effect on Nana Peg is instantaneous. She stops struggling, heck she even smiles a little. Frankie hopes she hasn't overdone it with the woman looking like she's been at the catnip. What's worse, blinded by anger, or stoned?

Frankie has to hold back her laughter when Dominik pats Zane on the shoulder. "Good job, my friend."

Zane puts his hand out, and the pair shakes on it over the top of Nana Peg. After helping each other to stand, they then assist Frankie's nana in getting to her feet. Okay, Frankie might have overdone it, just a teensy bit. At this rate the two alphas will be asking the guards if it's okay to knock them out.

"Blimmin' heck. You two stand over there." Frankie points to a spot next to a machine gun that hasn't received special attention from Dex. The men walk there as instructed. Zane even has his arm slung around the vampire's shoulders.

On feeling a nudge against the side of her leg, Frankie looks down to find Dex standing there. His head is tilted to the side in puzzlement. *"What's wrong with Zane and Dominik?"*

"Just a teensy little overdose. Watch this. It's gonna to be funny."

Frankie waves her wand in the direction of the pair, removing the calming spell. Any luck and they'll be back to normal in no time.

No sooner has the reversal taken force than Zane realizes he's virtually hugging Dominik. The vampire realizes at the same time, shrugging out of the merman's embrace. The disgust showing on both men's faces has Frankie slapping her hand over her mouth. The others don't bother hiding their laughter, with Nana Peg's having a 'tipsy' edge to it.

Frankie thinks briefly about reversing the spell on her nana too. Nope tipsy is better than a blinding anger likely to have her going off the deep end.

"Okay, enough messing about. Let's go through the plan again." She doesn't wait for a discussion on this. Instead Frankie bullet points the new elements they need to take into account, not least the top layer of prisoners.

"We do as we were going to before. We still take out the guards on the top level, but leave the prisoners where they are. It'll be safer for them this way."

Nana Peg waves her hand to get Frankie's attention. "I would prefer to release my sister now, than risk not being able to do so later."

Her nana has a good point.

Frankie's still adding up the pros and cons, when her nana speaks again. "What happens if we're not successful? I cannot leave my sister locked up, perhaps forever."

Frankie takes a second to think about it. As much as she doesn't want to contemplate failure, it's always a possibility.

"Okay, priority number one is release Selena. I'll take care of that." Better her nana doesn't know that A) she's been be-spelled and B) that Frankie plans on doing the same to her sister. Last thing they need is two fiery older ladies beating the living daylights out of William. Frankie wants that privilege.

Nana Peg already has her mouth open to argue the revised plan when Frankie holds her hand up. She's doing a lot of that these days. "Nana Peg, I need you to show the others around. I can help Selena on my own. As soon as she's free, we'll join you."

The one member of the team who won't be going down into the keep itself is Dex, and he is NOT happy about it. It takes all of Frankie's persuasive powers and even her using her 'Mom voice' to convince him. *"I need you up here, buddy. Otherwise I'll have no idea what William is up to. As soon as the mayhem starts, it'll be a matter of time before he sets fire to grandmamma and granddad."* Now there's something she never thought she'd say.

The team makes their way slowly down the stairs, speeding up once they're through the hologram and can see where they're putting their feet. Dex is the last to come through the mirage and he's dragging his feet. Even without his telepathic moaning Frankie would know he's not happy at being left behind.

"Come on, buddy, I need someone to watch my back. Without you up here I'd be going in blind." Frankie daren't talk up his new position any more than this. Gotta make it believable.

Dex sighs heavily before dropping in a heap on the first step clear of the hologram. Tucked away like he is he's got a good view of William and the bonfire from hell. He won't be easy to spot even if the concealment spell should falter. Frankie doesn't point out that this will only happen if she's hurt, or killed. No point scaring him if it's not necessary.

Sophie's already trotted down a couple of steps when she stops and returns. "Perhaps it would make sense if I stay up here too? It's the perfect spot to lob my babies down into the keep."

Sophie isn't talking infanticide, but rather tossing some of her flash explosives down into the courtyard. This will temporarily blind the guards and add to the general mayhem. Frankie knows confusion can be a good thing, especially when it's your team causing it.

"Good idea. No setting fire to Calico Jack and Anne. Well, not if you can help it."

Sophie hefts her backpack off her shoulders and dumps it on a step. "Pffft. Pity, because if ever there was a pair who deserved it, it's those two."

Frankie skips down the stairs, leaving the small witch lining up rum balls. The guards on the top level out cold courtesy of choke holds from Magda and Luca, her way forward is clear. The newly married couple work well together. There hasn't been a single squeak out of the guards up here or even from below. A quick look over the rails shows Dominik and Zane are likewise using sleeper holds.

This is good because it means William won't know they're here. If he did, it would be S'mores all round courtesy of her grandparents.

Frankie stands outside the cell and looks at the older woman floating within. There's no doubt this is her Aunt Selena in human form. Up close, the similarities between her and Nana Peg are startling. Could it be they're twins? Frankie's relieved to see her aunt appears in good health and has a rosy glow to her cheeks. It's something that's missing from the playmate in the cell next door.

Frankie doesn't bother calling out to Selena. Until she lifts her concealment spell, her aunt won't be able to hear her.

Frankie takes her wand and holds it up in the air, ready to stop the woman falling to the cell's hard granite floor. She's also going to include Selena in the team's camouflage spell. This way her great aunt will be able to communicate with Frankie and the others. It'll also mean she'll be invisible to William, his guards and any other inmates.

"Okay you two, am I good to go?"

There's a short pause before she gets a response from either.

"That's a go from me and Sophie, Mom."

"Hang on a second, Shortcake."

Frankie waits on Zane, tapping her toe. Suddenly having to stop when you're in the middle of all this havoc doesn't sit well.

"Yep, you're good to go. We just had to stop a group of guards who were heading your way."

Frankie has a quick look at the next level down and is met with the amazing site of Dominik and Zane standing side-by-side. *"You play nicely, now."* Frankie's unable to keep the laughter out of her telepathic message to the merman. She gets a telepathic snort in return.

Her thoughts are interrupted by a gleeful shout of, *"Go Mom, go!"* from Dex. There's more than a hint of cheerleader about it.

Frankie 'goes' as he's instructed. She runs her left hand across the front of the force field that fronts Selena's cell. Thanks to her Wereall bloodline it disappears allowing her to enter. Something else that drops is Selena, with her no longer held in suspension. Luckily Frankie has been expecting this, stopping the woman just short of the granite floor. She'd learned the hard way when on opening her dad's cell he'd dropped like a bag of cement.

Her aunt still comfortably floating, Frankie ignores the yelling and screaming from the levels below her. Their plan to take William unawares is obviously out the window. She hits her aunt with a becalming spell designed to help on two levels. Firstly, the woman will be able to come to terms with having been locked up. Secondly, it'll stop her from rushing off to throttle her cheating spouse. On seeing the gleam around the woman, Frankie knows she's safely covered by the team's concealment spell.

Everything in place, Frankie lowers the woman gently to the ground, then helps her to stand.

"What happened? What am I doing in here? The last thing I remember is having dinner in New York with William."

There's no way Frankie's breaking the news now. "I'm not sure. We're here to free innocents. I was passing, and I saw you in here. I didn't think you should be." Okay so this is a lie, but it's a white one.

"Mom, William's lit the match! I repeat he's lit the match."

"Listen Selena, it's going to get a little crazy here. Let's get you up to your room. I'll come get you when it calms down."

This has the woman nodding woodenly in response. Okay, Frankie's perhaps added a bit much 'obedience' to that calming spell. There'll be plenty of time later for the woman to get even with William. In the middle of a battle is most definitely not the place.

"Mom! Mom, he's dropped the match."

15

Frankie's ready to transport herself to William's side and take the matches away along with his hand, when Dex continues.

"He missed the kindling. Oooh, oooh. He burned his fingers. Hah! Now he's sucking on them."

Frankie can't help but join in with her small pup's snickering. It serves the odious man right. *"See, I told you I needed you up there. Let me know if you see flames."*

No point in Frankie panicking prematurely. Dex is more than capable of this on his own. She also knows Zane will let her know if she needs to act urgently. Part of her is loath to free Calico Jack and Anne. Those two would be bound to mess up the latest version of the team's plan. Better they stay put.

Even though it's a short walk to the stairs that lead to the private quarters, Frankie avoids it. Better her aunt doesn't get to see the other inmates on the top level. There's no way Frankie can explain away this many scantily clad, surgically enhanced prisoners. Sheesh, talk about your Silicon Valley.

A casual wave of her wand and they're in Selena's room. Frankie's making sure the woman is comfy in her bed when Dex's words explode inside her head.

"I see flames! I repeat... I see flames!"

"Shortcake, you're out of time. If you're doing something, you need to do it now."

Even if the pair hadn't reported this, Calico Jack and Anne's yelling and screaming has told her something is up. "Not on my watch you don't."

Selena's brow creases. "Sorry, what is it you don't want me to do?"

Frankie pats her aunt's hand. "Oh, nothing, I was just talking to myself. Why don't you have a nap and I'll be back to check on you soon?" Her question is rhetorical, she knows Selena will obey, at least until the spell wears off.

Dex yelling out, *"Fire! Fire!"* has her spinning around and flying back down the stairs. She meets up with Nana Peg in the doorway to the courtyard. "Selena's safe. She's upstairs."

Frankie has to stop her nana from going to join her sister. "Nana, we need you to open the cells as a distraction. I need to take care of saving my grandparents."

Her nana appears torn between her duty to her sister and wanting to help Frankie. Eventually, much to Frankie's relief, she turns away from the stairs. The guards on the ninth level unconscious thanks to Luca and Magda, Peggy heads there. She moves quickly for an older woman. As she passes each cell, she swipes her hand across the front. This breaks the barrier, releasing the prisoner from suspension. The sound of bodies hitting the ground and groaning follows in her wake.

Happy her nana is busy; Frankie takes a quick look down into the courtyard. Hmmm, Dex's calls of 'fire, fire' appear to have been a little premature. William still fumbling with the matches says the fire hasn't taken hold properly. She's got time!

Frankie transports herself to the level below her Nana Peg before mimicking the woman's actions. Because Frankie's faster, perhaps due to that smidge of vampire in her system, she finishes her level in under a minute. She then moves to the next level down, all while keeping a wary eye on William.

She doesn't want him to know exactly what's happening until she and the others are good and ready. Sure the prisoners moaning and groaning tell him the shields that front the cells are falling, but this is all. Of interest is that neither he nor his imperial guards appear keen on investigating what's going on. The guards in particular stay in formation next to the fire, barely moving a muscle.

Frankie wonders if William is staying where he is because of the 'muscle' surrounding him. Only on comparing these guards to the rank and file in the keep does she realize how freaking big they are. They have to be at least a head taller than any of the others, and way taller than William. Seven feet tall is her conservative estimate.

Frankie's about to swipe her hand across the front of the next cell she comes to when she stills. No way? It can't be. She shakes her head to clear her vision. It didn't need it because she's still seeing the same thing. Without any further warnings from Dex, Frankie takes her time to examine the woman floating before her.

White curly hair? Check!

Plump, rosy cheeks? Check!

Pleasantly rounded? Check!

If Frankie didn't know better, she'd say the woman floating in front of her is her Aunt Betty. She's basing this on the woman's uncanny resemblance to the gorgeous Betty White.

"Hang on a second. If you're in here, who's behind all that mayhem on the island? Or have you just arrived?"

Frankie's torn. Does she slide her hand across the front of the cell or move on leaving the woman safely locked up? The woman will be none the wiser if she does.

She's not willing to take the chance that she might not be around to free her potential aunt later. Wand in her right hand, she slides her other across the invisible barrier. In an instant the woman falls.

Frankie's just as quick to twitch her wand. This both includes the woman in the team's cover-up spell and stops her inches off the hard granite. It's been closer than Frankie would like, but better than the alternative.

The woman blinks her eyes, confusion clouding her features. "But I've not been in place in eons. How can I be back here? Who are you?"

It's a second before her Aunt Betty's words coalesce in Frankie's mind. The older lady has been here before? Surely she isn't one who got it on with a Wereall guard? No, she can't be, that member of the family was, or is, a direct descendent of Calico Jack and Anne Bonny. Frankie's fiery locks confirm this.

Something else that's a surprise is the woman's voice. It has Frankie fighting the urge to pull her elderly relation in for a tight hug. The desire to do so is almost irresistible. She's not once felt this with Calico Jack and Anne Bonny. It's something that has Frankie feeling whole for the first time since her mom was murdered. Not even finding her dad alive had brought about this feeling of completion.

On hearing more shouting from the courtyard and inside her head, Frankie knows there isn't time to explain what's going on. She steps inside the cell and grabs the woman's ankle. A wave of peace rolls over her, swamping her with love and kindness. Frankie has to fight the tears that threaten. She doesn't have time for this now. Another wave of her wand and they're in Selena's bedroom at the top of the tower. As instructed her aunt is on the bed, having a nap.

"You'll be safe here. I'll come get you when everything dies down."

Frankie positions the woman over the bed and lowers her into place.

"I'll explain everything later. Right now I have to stop a barbeque."

Unable to hold back any longer, Frankie drags the woman into a tight hug and squeezes hard. The emotions that swamp her are close to overwhelming. It also confirms two things for her. Firstly, the woman is devoid of any magic. Secondly, she's also devoid of any evil.

"Are you okay, Shortcake? Your brain is in overdrive."

"I'm... I'm fine."

Frankie pulls herself free of her Aunt Betty's arm, not bothering to leave the room the old-fashioned way. Rather than return to her previous location, she arrives on the Level 6 walkway. It's immediately obvious none of the team with their sleeper holds have been here. The guard standing next to Frankie is very much awake. He also doesn't have a clue she's right next to him. Frankie's not a fan of the sleeper hold. There's too much up-close-and-personal for her liking.

Instead she hits him with a sleeper spell. It works as well and is just as quiet. She even stops him hitting the walkway to avoid unwanted grunting. Best not to alert the guards spread out on either side of them.

A whiff of smoke has her looking down into the keep. Sure enough the kindling at the very base of the teetering pile of wood is alight. It's not exactly roaring. But, if Frankie was roped to a pole in the middle like her grandparents are, she'd be yelling too. Does she have time to incapacitate all the guards on this level though? That's the question.

After reciting an incantation in her head, Frankie sweeps her wand around the whole level, hitting the guards, one after the other. It's like a Wereall game of skittles so quickly does it all happen.

Frankie turns to check the inmate behind her and is amazed to see an empty cell. This makes a nice change. Did someone get out on good behavior? She's not letting it go to waste.

Frankie unclips her silver bat earrings and tosses them into the granite grotto that is the cell. She then swipes her hand across the front of the space. She's wondering if this is enough to seal the space back up, when her bat earrings flash brightly. Cool, it's worked!

Dracul and Natasha back in their human forms glare at her, even baring their fangs. The rebellion doesn't last long. Their eyelids flutter closed and they assume the state of suspended animation common to all the inmates. Apart that is from those who've been released and are stalking the upper levels like zombies.

The prisoners are just like her dad had been on release and are keeping the guards busy exactly as per their plan. As fast as the prisoners are locked back in their cells, Nana Peg frees them again. It's like a multi-level game of *Whac-a-Mole*.

"*Mom, the fire's getting bigger.*"

Frankie hasn't needed this panicked reminder. The smoke swirling around the courtyard is getting thicker by the second. Her grandparents' screaming is also escalating. This is soon replaced by strangled coughing. Blast them mucking up the plan Frankie and the others had cobbled together atop the keep.

She throws a silencing spell around her head, giving her the quiet she needs to think.

"*Shortcake! Behind you.*" Frankie spins on the spot and is faced with a guard sprinting in her direction, her response is automatic. A brief wave of her wand and he's on his way to taking a much needed bath.

"*Thank you.*" And thank the Goddess her silence spell hadn't stopped Zane's warning from getting to her.

"Of course, that's it!" If she can send the guards out into the ocean, surely she can bring the ocean to the imperial guards dotted around William and the bonfire? A moment's thought and she spreads her arms wide, focusing her energies on the incantation.

> *God of the depths,*
> *please listen to me.*
> *Send me your waves,*
> *send me your sea.*
> *Rinse out the poison,*
> *damp down the flame.*
> *Send me your spawn,*
> *it's such that I claim.*

Okay, it's a little hokey, but it's gonna have to do. She waves her wand around the cardinal points and then toward the bonfire below her. For a second nothing happens. Then the middle of the keep is inundated with seawater, complete with a couple of sharks and even a giant squid. Ooops, perhaps 'spawn' wasn't the right word?

"*Hah! I don't think William likes sushi.*"

Dex has a point. William, who's treading water next to the sodden bonfire, is definitely not a fan of fresh seafood. Especially when it's a six-foot shark, that's circling him like he's lunch. The giant squid slapping him around the head with a tentacle doesn't look like fun either.

It doesn't look as if the imperial guards are keen on intercepting either. To a Wereall they've scaled the bonfire leaving William to look after himself. Frankie can see demotions in their future.

Much as it would be fun to see the murderous Wereall taken out like this, Frankie's conscious of the water draining away through cracks in the stonework. She doesn't want to be responsible for hurting living beings, even those with big teeth and tentacles. Another wave of her wand and she sends them back home.

She's achieved her goal of saving her grandparents from immolation, but do they appear grateful? Not likely. Anne in particular looks as grumpy as usual, her red hair hanging in tails down her face.

Calico Jack glances all around as though in search of their rescuer. He stares right through Frankie before his gaze returns. She's in no doubt that on some level he can sense her, just as William had done earlier. Is the cover-up spell she's placed on the team failing?

There's one way to be sure.

A quick flick of her wrist and the imperial guard still perched on the bonfire are sent over the wall and far out into the sea. Guess they're going for a swim after all. Frankie transports herself to a spot directly in front of her grandparents. There's no reaction from either of them.

She decides to push her test further.

"Can either of you see or hear me?"

There isn't a peep out of them. However, Calico Jack's breathing deepening tells her he's aware someone is near. Is he sensing this, or is it all down to the wood pile moving under Frankie's feet?

Fairly confident, the concealment spell is still in place; Frankie calls out to her nana.

"Nana Peg, you can stop opening those cells." The Goddess knows what sort of criminals they've already released as a result of their diversion. There hadn't exactly been time to scan each prisoner before releasing them. Her nana stops immediately, spins on her heel and makes for the doorway leading to Selena's room in the tower.

Good, much better if the older members of their team are out the way of any physical confrontations. It'll also give those guards still on their feet, time to get the remaining prisoners locked up again.

While the three vampires and Zane have taken out a lot of the Wereall guards, more and more stream into the keep. Mayhap word got back to the barracks that they were needed? Shame Frankie hadn't thought to seal the doors as she had last time they were here. It's something she rectifies immediately stopping any further reinforcements from gaining entry.

In her defense the humongous fire in the middle of the keep threw her. Frankie ignores the guards swarming around the bonfire; instead pointing her wand at the miles of rope that secures her grandparents. Nothing happens. The knots stay as tight as ever, despite her grandparents struggling mightily.

"That's odd."

She knows her magic is working here, so why not now? Have the knots been spelled? The question is who's responsible. She thought she was the only one at the keep with magical powers. She hadn't picked up anything magical emanating from her Aunt Betty, except for that weird connection of theirs.

The one thing Frankie can do for her grandparents to protect them is include them in the spell as she's done with Selena and Betty. This will also have the bonus of her grandparents knowing they're indebted to her. As dishonest and conniving as they are, she knows they'll honor a debt like this. You just never knew when you'd need to cash in.

Frankie comes close to smacking herself on the side of the head. She can't believe she's thinking like they do. It would appear the witchy apple doesn't fall far from the family tree.

Her mind made up, she waves her wand, including her grandparents and all that rope in the cover-up spell. A couple of things tell Frankie she's been successful.

Firstly, there's a roar from the guards that their prisoners have disappeared before their very eyes. Secondly Anne and Jack both impale Frankie with looks of disgust. She knows why, and it's enough to have her breaking into a broad grin.

"You both owe me. Big time!"

Not that the pair is home-free just yet. Actually they're not free at all with the knots refusing to budge magically or otherwise. Perhaps it is better they stay where they are for now? The last thing Frankie needs is them running loose in the keep. Unless?

"Shortcake, don't even think about it. You don't have time. Leave them for now, they'll be okay."

Zane's right. Even if she hurried she'd be away for longer than is safe. There's also the risk she'll arrive back before she arrived the first time. And boy doesn't that whole time slip thing do her head in.

Nope, she's here to save the innocent, not help the guilty. They're staying tightly lashed to the stake, for now, at least.

It's on turning to grab William that she realizes he's no longer in the courtyard.

While there are many options for places he could have gone, she instinctively knows where he is. Bang goes the theory of keeping the older members of the family away from danger.

16

Rather than transport herself directly into the turret bedchamber, Frankie materializes at the bottom of the stairs. If she can eavesdrop, she should be able to get some idea of what's going on. Better this than suddenly arriving and facing who knew what.

She wouldn't put it past William to hold her aunt and nana hostage, using a blunderbuss if the machine guns up top are anything to go by.

Frankie's unable to stop thoughts of some weird prisoner exchange taking place. To Frankie's way of thinking the older women upstairs are worth half a dozen silicon dollies apiece, if not more. Doubtless William will be after a better exchange rate than this.

His escaping isn't an option. If he's happy to deal with the likes of the Garnets and Mimi Merriweather, that's a big fat NO.

Surely that New York penthouse must cost a

stack of cash to maintain. This has to increase the chances of him striking a deal with someone else. Frankie twists her head from side to side, loosening her neck muscles. As relaxed as she's likely to get, she sneaks up the winding granite stairway. She's near the top when she hears a familiar voice. It's one that has her blood chilling in her veins.

It can't be. How can that even be possible? She can't be here.

"What? What's happening, Mom? Who are you talking about?"

"Shortcake, everything okay?"

"Shhh you two, I can't hear myself think."

Their chattering also makes it impossible to listen in on the conversation taking place in the turret room. The pair finally on mute, Frankie concentrates again. She plasters herself against the curved wall and then risks inching up a couple more steps. Her hand strays to the pocket of her coat and she slides her wand free. She's going to need it. Or will she? It might be more fun without it. There's nothing so energizing as taking out the trash the old-school way.

This sees her sliding the silver wand up the sleeve of her coat where it's less likely to be damaged. A couple of quick breaths and she sneaks up the final half dozen stairs and into the turret room itself. Courtesy of the concealment spell, the pair at the side of the bed has no idea she's arrived.

Frankie takes in what's happening at a glance. Nana Peg stands behind William, a bed pan raised above her head ready to bean him. Only she doesn't. It takes Frankie another second to realize her nana is frozen in place. No doubt courtesy of the woman standing next to the Wereall leader at the side of the bed.

On the plus side, William and his friend don't have a clue there are two women in the large bed that dominates the room. On making eye contact with her Selena and Betty, Frankie puts her fingers to her lips and holds her hand up. She gets brief nods in return confirming they know to keep still. Even though they're invisible, if they move so will the mountain of blankets.

Despite having recognised the woman's voice from downstairs, Frankie has to shake her head to center her scattered thoughts. It shouldn't even be possible. She looks from her Aunt Betty in the bed to her doppelganger standing next to William. If not for the two women being in the same room, she'd have been taken in by Gwen Morris for sure.

Never mind Stanley's evil daughter doesn't look as Frankie remembers, she shouldn't even be a woman. She should be a lizard hanging out in a nice warm terrarium back in Seattle. But, if she's here, then where's Stanley? Is he even alive because Frankie wouldn't put patricide past Gwen. The witch is evil to the core, just like her Succubus mother, Mimi Merriweather. It's this she-devil whose powers swirl in Frankie's system. That her daughter has inherited her mother's evil is in no doubt.

Frankie has to admit Gwen has done a bang-up job of impersonating her Aunt Betty. There's one difference so far as she can see. Her real Aunt Betty huddled under the covers, isn't wearing an amulet. The witch pretending to be her, most definitely is.

At a sub-cellular level Frankie knows the amulet worn by Gwen Morris is the very one used by the mystery man at the cliff face. Surely it must be booby trapped to cause that sort of damage? Might even be fun to get Gwen to have a go at using it. Pity Frankie doesn't have time to find out.

Her evil thoughts are disturbed by Zane speaking to her telepathically. *"What's she doing there?"*

That he's picked on Frankie's scattered thoughts is no surprise. However, it's an unwelcome distraction, but one she'll need to deal with.

"Not sure. I'll let you know as soon as I find out."

"You need any help?"

"Nah, I'll be good. I've learned a lot since I last tangled with the creature."

However, Frankie's first target isn't Gwen. It's

William. Even with Gwen able access her magic, it's not easy hexing someone you can't see. And Frankie plans on moving around, A LOT.

She starts with a sweeping sidekick that sees William collapsing in a heap on the floor. Frankie follows him down; immediately dragging him into a nasty wrestling hold Zane taught her. It's one that has the Wereall Commander yelling in surrender and even slapping the ground. If Frankie was after subjugation this would be great. She's not.

She'll be happy with nothing more than seeing him locked up in one of his own cells, for good!

She's applying pressure when the Oriental rug beside her explodes in a cloud of singed wool. Jinxed jellyfish that was close! Too close. Bang goes her theory of being safe from being hexed while she's invisible. A quick twist of her hips and Frankie's got the Wereall between her and anything flying out the end of Gwen's wand.

Frankie tightens her arm around his neck, squeezing until he slumps in her arms. He's not dead, just out cold. It's far easier to transport him this way than if he's struggling. She's going to have to hit Gwen with something that will have her unconscious too.

But first, she's got questions that need answers.

Frankie jumps to her feet, dodging a couple

more hexes in the process. A quick jerk of her arm and her wand shoots down the sleeve of her coat and into her outstretched hand.

"Immobilis!" The effect on Gwen is instantaneous. She stands statue-like, ready to fire another hex at Frankie. Phew, that was close. If Frankie hadn't frozen the women when she did, the hex would have scored a direct hit.

"How dare you!" The anger showing in Gwen's eyes is lethal in the extreme. Her gaze swiveling back and forth confirms she definitely can't see Frankie.

"Oh, I dare alright." Frankie pokes Gwen in the chest and is delighted to watch her fall like an ironing board onto the bed. It's something that has Selena and Betty scrambling to get their feet out of the way.

The evil witch incapacitated, Frankie lifts the concealment spell that has hidden her identity. The merest wave of her wand above her head and she pops into view.

Selena, Betty and Peg, however, remain hidden.

"You!" spits out Gwen, although she appears to regret this. "My darling niece, I've been so worried about you." Even her voice has changed. It's softer and has more in keeping with Frankie's actual relation.

Unbelievable! The horrid woman's trying to maintain the charade even jinxed as she is. As tempting as it is to have some fun with this, Frankie simply can't be bothered. She's going to nip it in the bud right now.

"Nice try... Gwen."

"Gwen?" Who's Gwen?"

"Oh, give it up, would you? You're not my Aunt Betty. I've already met her, ah, downstairs." No point revealing her aunt's current location mere inches away.

With it obvious the gig is up, Gwen rolls her eyes in the only expression available to her. "And so what happens now you nasty little ginger?"

That this is said in Gwen's normal voice adds to the sting of the insult. It takes every ounce of Frankie's resolve not to flatten the woman. No one calls her ginger. Heck even her dad calling her *Pumpkin* is borderline.

"I'll start with something easy. Did you kill the security guards back at *Garnet Cove*?"

Gwen doesn't even bother trying to deny it. She even sounds proud of how easy it was to achieve their demise. "They were in the way, they had to go. The funniest was trapping your odious grandfather and that concubine of his." Gwen cackles delightedly before spitting out how she'd done so. Frankie has to admit brushing sleeping potion on all the steak in the fridge had been clever.

Could it simply be the murders on the island were to avoid anyone getting in the way of Gwen and her power grab? From Frankie's experience with the witch it would certainly be true to form. Gwen didn't give a jot about collateral damage. Heck, she even reveled in it.

"What have you done to Stanley?" While the old guy might cramp Frankie's style at times, she's got a bit of a soft spot for him. She'd hate to think of him being taken out by this odious creature.

"Hah, my stupid father was lonely. Didn't take much to convince him we could have a lovely catch-up if I was back being a human. I promised to behave."

Frankie's eyes widen. "And he believed you?"

"Yes!" crows Gwen. "How stupid is he?"

Frankie lifts a brow a-la-Zane. "Hmmmph, it must be hereditary."

Gwen's eyes narrow. If she could move right now, Frankie would be so dead.

No sooner has this thought skipped across Frankie's mind than the woman does exactly this. She rears up off the bed, her wand pointed at Frankie's heart, death in her eyes.

"Are you freaking kidding me?" The question is rhetorical, with Frankie not expecting an answer. If magic isn't going to hold up against Gwen, she knows her Jeet Kune Do skills will. She power kicks Gwen's wand out of her hand not caring if she breaks fingers in the process. This sees it flying across the room with sparks shooting out the end. Luckily they miss anything and anyone. The last thing they need is a fire; even if the room is cold enough Frankie can see her breath.

Gwen isn't going down without a fight. Her hands curl into claws, her French-manicured nails aiming for Frankie's face. Frankie easily deflects Gwen's talons. A quick step to the side and she's got the older woman in a headlock, and not just any headlock. It's one that should put a stop to the woman swamping her, or any of the others, with black magic. Frankie only needs exert a little pressure and it'll be lights out. But, before this she wants answers.

"What have you done with Stanley?"

The woman remains mute, forcing Frankie to increase the pressure.

"I said... what have... you done... with Stanley?"

She punctuates her question with a few extra-tight squeezes. The final one has Gwen grunting.

"I'm sorry, what was that?" Frankie does a double squeeze. "You'll need to speak up, I can't hear you."

"I jinxed him and drained his powers when his back was turned. Then I used a portal in the marina to travel here. The stupid man doesn't know there's one right on his doorstep." Laughter once again gets the better of Gwen. No longer manic, the witch's laughter is full-on psychotic.

Hexed harridans. Like mother, like daughter.

That there's a portal to the realm of the We-reall close by the marina is news to Frankie and it sounds as if she isn't alone. This must be how William turned up on their doorstep when he did. It also explains how it is that Gwen was at *Garnet Cove* before them even though she left the marina after they did. As concerning as all this is, it's a worry for another day.

"And Calico Jack, what did you do to him?"

Gwen doesn't speak although her peals of laughter are answer enough. The one way Jack could be trussed up like he is, is if Gwen siphoned his powers while he was out cold. This also makes the evil woman twice as strong as she ever was. Add Stanley's powers to the mix and the woman is close to formidable. It also explains why she was able to break through Frankie's Immobilis spell.

Frankie knows what she needs to do. Question is will she be able to give Jack and Stanley back their energy when it comes time. She still hasn't got the hang of keeping the different energies separate. Instead they swirl together inside her with no beginning and no end.

Frankie keeps up the pressure on Gwen's neck. As tempting as it is to handle the problem herself, there might be a safer way. To know for sure she's going to need to remove the concealment spell.

A wave of her hand and Selena is visible

along with Nana Peg and the real Aunt Betty. A gasp from Gwen tells of her also being able to see the two women in the bed.

Selena, who stares at her sister, appears a world away. She then stumbles out of bed and over to Nana Peg's side. She tries pulling her sisters arms back down to her sides to no avail. She does however manage to wrench the bed warmer from her sister's grasp. For a second Frankie thinks the woman is going to use it, instead she flings it to one side with a clatter.

"Selena, I'll sort her out in a minute. First, I've got to deal with this one." Frankie tightens her hold to get Gwen back under control. "Would it be possible to strap this pile of slime into the *Syphonia* and retrieve Stanley and Jack's energy?"

The woman creases her forehead. She stays like this for a second or two before speaking. "While it's possible, I don't know what I'm doing and I'm unsure of the loyalties of those who can run the *Syphonia*. There was a time when I could do so myself with it being as natural as breathing. Alas those days are long gone."

This leaves Frankie with no option.

17

Closing her eyes, Frankie concentrates on the energy swirling in and around Gwen's struggling form. There's no denying Gwen's magical footprint is what she picked up around the resort. No wonder it was familiar with a good portion of it down to Stanley and possibly even Calico Jack.

Frankie doesn't draw on it, rather she 'tastes' it, trying to identify Stanley and Jack's unique signatures from all the others. And yes there are a lot of other energies mixed in there. Gwen really does follow in her mother's footsteps when it comes to taking power from others.

As tempting as it is to take away any energy that doesn't belong to the old witch, Frankie resists. She doesn't want to be encumbered with all sorts of evil powers. Being lumbered with Mimi Merriweather's demonic powers is enough thank you very much. No, this time it's a case of Stanley and her granddad's powers or nothing.

"Shortcake, what are you up to?"

Even though Zane has spoken inside her head, she knows he's right behind her. Not that she can see him, with him still being invisible to her. Weirdly she gets that Dex is with him.

"Sorry, Mom. I was worried about you."

"That's okay, buddy. I might need some help here."

A quick wave of her wand and she and the three older women can actually see the new arrivals. "She's taken Stanley and CJ's powers. We can't use the *Syphonia* and I'm not locking up their powers with her."

Zane's brows knot in worry. "Stanley's powers?"

Frankie gives him a quick update on what Gwen has been up to. It's something that has him frowning mightily.

"Are you sure you can keep control of all that power?"

Frankie doesn't hesitate before giving him an emphatic nod. Fake it 'til you make it. Isn't that how it goes? "Yep, I just need to think of them as separate entities. That way I'll be able to compartmentalize them. It'll make it easier to return it to them later."

That's if she does return her granddad's powers. Powered up he's a menace. Unfortunately without them, he's most likely dead. Surely it's his magic keeping him alive after all these years? He had after all been 'hanged until dead' because of his pirating ways. The reason her grandmamma had escaped the noose was because she'd been pregnant with Frankie's great, great, great, whatever at the time.

Someone who isn't dead is Gwen, with the woman struggling ever harder against Frankie's hold. If she keeps this up, Frankie won't have a hope of focusing on the energies swilling around in the woman's system.

"Zane, can you hit her with an immobilis spell?"

She doesn't need to ask him twice, with him pointing his wand at the squirming witch seconds later. Light streaks out the end of the wooden sliver, hitting Gwen right between the eyes. Frankie would even think the woman had expired from the strike if not for being able to feel her carotid pulse thrumming with life. Oh well, never mind.

The witch rigid, it's an easy thing for Frankie to trace the coven leader's stolen powers.

"Gotcha!" Stanley's power tingles up Frankie's arm before it's reclaimed by Gwen. Even frozen as she is, she's still stopping Frankie's attempts at retrieval. "Oh, no you don't, you evil crone." Frankie tightens her grip around the woman's neck. She keeps the pressure on until the witch goes limp in her arms.

Frankie then lays the witch down on the rug next to William and places her hand on the woman's forehead. Her palm is flat and her fingers widespread. It takes a second or two before she latches onto Stanley's power again. It's akin to getting olives out of the jar using your fingers.

However, once it starts, the transfer is relatively straightforward. Rather than let it meld with her own, Frankie contains the coven leader's powers. She even visualizes a small safe with *Stanley* written on the front.

It works. Rather than merge with hers, the coven leader's powers speed straight into the small metal box. The last few drops carefully contained, Frankie metaphorically slams the door shut and spins the lock.

"That wasn't so bad. Okay granddad let's get you out of this nasty piece of work."

Frankie isn't sure why she's speaking to Calico Jack's stolen powers. Perhaps it's because Stanley's had felt so much like a living thing.

"Are you sure about this, Shortcake?"

Again, Frankie nods, while doing her best to keep a tight lid on the thoughts of failure that are sloshing around in her head. "Just keep an eye on Gwen. If it looks like she's coming around or your spell is failing, jinx her again."

Frankie goes back to concentrating on the

powers in Gwen's system. Her locating those belonging to her Calico Jack is proving a lot harder. She'll latch onto them only to have them slip away. When she finds them again, they somehow feel different. She's even having second thoughts about collecting them when they shoot up her arm without warning.

She's nowhere ready for them. No little metal box waiting to hold them. No chance of containment at all. Frankie drops back onto her heels, her vision clouded by sparkling lights. The buzzing that surrounds and fills her head is akin to a thousand angry bees. Her heart is ready to claw its way free of her chest.

"Mom, what's wrong?"

"Nothing, Dex. I'm all good." Her telepathic response is stuttered.

"You don't sound all good. You don't look so good, either."

Hmmm, the Jack Russell might have a point. Not entirely unexpected though with essence of Calico Jack flooding her system. She's vaguely aware of Zane dragging her into his arms and hugging her tight. The desire to yell 'Arrrgh, me hearties,' and swish a cutlass around is something that has her giggling. In her current state Frankie suspects she could even give Anne Bonny a run for her money.

It happens slowly, but eventually the buzzing subsides and her vision clears. Then she feels invincible, unfortunately in an evil-overload kinda way. Excellent, it'll come in handy for dealing with the two good-for-nothings sprawled on the floor in front of her.

The first thing she does is reinstate the concealment spell on everyone in the room, except William and Gwen. She's thought about including them and had then decided against it. No point making an example of them if no-one can see the result.

"Hang fire, ladies. I'll be back soon."

Selena turns from her examination of Nana Peg. "Wait, where are you taking him?" The woman's voice is tinged with concern.

"I'm gonna lock him up, if that's okay with you?"

Her Wereall aunt smiles broadly. "The longer the better. It's about time my family regained control of this realm."

Frankie takes this piece of information on board, making a mental note to ask Selena or Nana Peg about it later. Could it be that William married above his station and not the other way around? She'd never have guessed this from Selena's previously subservient nature.

"I won't be long." Frankie checks she's in contact with William and Gwen, and is ready to wave her wand around the three of them when Selena yells 'stop'.

Frankie's hand drops to her side. "What's

wrong? I thought you wanted me to lock him up?"

"I do, but you're not locking this evil woman up with her powers still in place." Selena drops to her knees next to Gwen's inert form. She then carefully places one hand on Gwen's forehead and her other on the witch's solar plexus. "Best you stand back, I'm a little rusty."

Frankie doesn't need to be asked twice, knowing what it is Selena's about to do. She wants to be well back in case the powers spill over, or worse, escape completely. Likewise Zane has moved away, dragging Dex with him.

The first thing Frankie becomes aware of is the low-level hum. Then she watches in amazement as Selena starts to glow. While this starts out mildly enough, the woman is soon bright enough that Frankie has to shield her eyes.

Frankie's thinking it can't get any brighter in the room when there's an audible pop and the light disappears. By comparison the room feels dark, but not so dark that Frankie doesn't see Nana Peg's arms slicing through the air. If she'd still be armed with the bed warmer, she'd have flattened her sister.

Only after her eyes have readjusted is Frankie able to look at Gwen properly. The woman looks deflated somehow and even though her eyes are wide open, Frankie gets the impression there's no-one home. She is so not telling Stanley about this.

"You got that right, Shortcake. This stays between us."

Frankie leans down and touches the amulet that sits tight against Gwen's throat. No soon has she done so than the clasp pops open, allowing her to lift it free. She then hands it over to her Aunt Betty. "I believe this is yours?"

Betty takes hold of the charm and is all fingers and thumbs when she puts it back around her own neck. "Thank you, I don't even remember losing it. I don't remember much at all and certainly not how I found my way back here."

Frankie adds asking her Aunt Betty about that side of the family history to a long list. In the meantime she needs to take out the trash. Once again she makes sure she's in contact with William and Gwen. "I'll see you back downstairs." She then waves her wand efficiently not giving Zane a chance to join her.

Their first stop is the top level of cells. A quick check over the guard rail shows her grandparents remain lashed to the stake atop the pile of soggy firewood.

Good, she's still not sure what she's going to do with them. It might be better for all concerned if she held onto her granddad's powers. That this could put an end to his half-life has her immediately crossing that option off the list. Could it be she can give him enough power to keep him alive, but not enough that he can cause pandemonium? A quick scan of all the cells and Frankie spots the perfect one. It's the same one William had locked Selena in and it's got a brilliant view of Silicon Valley.

Frankie points her wand at William and he's levitating a moment later. A quick flick of her wrist sees him flying into the cell. He hits the back wall hard and drops to the ground in a heap. Ooops, she hadn't meant to move him quite so rapidly. Oh well, never mind.

The one thing she's got to ensure is that once she's locked William up, he stays that way. Instead of locking his cell with her Wereall powers, she hexes it to within an inch of HIS life. This way, no matter how hard the imperial guards try, they won't be able to release him. They'll be able to slide food, bedding and a bucket into him, but that'll be it. No spending years in suspended animation for him. He's going to be aware of every single second of his prison term.

The Wereall leader being incarcerated here is poetic justice of the highest order. Shame she can't leave the bounty of beauties for him to look at but not touch. As devious as this would be, it wouldn't be fair on the women. They're just as innocent as a lot of the other prisoners in here, perhaps even more so.

Frankie drops to the next level and stuffs Gwen in the nearest empty cell. She then runs her hand across the front of the space, reinstating the Wereall barrier. This sees Gwen floating up into the middle of the cell, safely suspended and in a dream like state. As much as the woman needs a fate far worse, Frankie knows hearing of this would destroy Stanley. He's going to have enough trouble dealing with his daughter being locked up here in the first place.

Frankie repeats the hex that will make it impossible for anyone other than her to release the woman. No time off for good behavior for her. No time off, full stop. Doing so is probably overkill with Selena having stripped Gwen of all her powers. Normally this would be enough for Frankie. But, having seen first-hand Gwen's ability to keep on coming back to life, she's not risking it.

"Right, it's time to free the innocent." No sooner has she said this to herself than the sensation of ants crawling over her stops. Her sigh is heartfelt.

EPILOGUE

Hours of tedium follow. The last thing Frankie expected during this adventure was to be bored out of her brain.

One by one the prisoners are released from their cells and presented to Selena as she walks slowly around each level. Gone is the subservient woman Frankie is used to. It might be the crown or the floor-length ermine cape that covers a dress of gold brocade.

Someone who's awestruck by the new and improved Selena is Dex. He stares open mouthed at her watching her every move. He doesn't stay quiet for long. *"Mom, does this mean you're a princess?"*

It takes a second for his question to worm its way through the myriad of thoughts about things she'd rather be doing. "What?"

"If Selena is a queen, doesn't that make you a princess, like Nana Peg?"

Frankie opens her mouth to answer, but nothing comes out. She isn't sure she knows. Eventually he stops his worship of Selena long enough to turn and look at her, his expression is expectant.

"I'm, I'm not sure." And Frankie isn't. It's a question for another day.

"I hope you are. Prince Dex sounds cool, don't ya think?"

It takes all Frankie's willpower to stop her burst of laughter in its tracks. She even puts a lid on her telepathic snorting, just in case. No point bursting the small pup's ambitious bubble.

Zane and Dominik drag another prisoner in front of Selena and she places her hand on the inmate's forehead and scans them.

Thanks to Selena's bloodline, she's able to sense who should stay and who should go. It's a shame Nana Peg hasn't inherited this ability like her sister. It would be a lot faster with two of them.

At this stage it's working out at 80/20 in favor of the bad guys. There are a lot more of them in here than Frankie realized. Even so, the *Syphonia* will be running overtime restoring power to any inmates who've been wrongly imprisoned.

Someone who's already had their magical powers returned is her Aunt Betty. Frankie had thought it was Mimi who'd stripped Betty of her powers. Turns out it was Gwen, the evil daughter.

Once this was confirmed, it had been a straightforward matter for Selena to transfer them from herself.

The process complete, Selena had gently put her hand on Frankie's shoulder. "If you like I could rid you of the essence of the Succubus that clouds your system."

Frankie stiffens. She isn't sure if she likes it that Selena has scanned her without permission. She also isn't sure she wants anyone messing about with her powers. Who knew what removal of demon influences would do to her fledgling powers? "If it's okay with you, I'll hang onto them for now. They're not causing me any issues."

Selena does nothing to hide her surprise as this assertion from Frankie, leaving Frankie to wonder what it is she should be dealing with. Is there another nasty Succubus style surprise waiting in the wings? She hopes not.

Even with Betty once again empowered, the connection between Frankie and her aunt remains strong. Frankie has no idea why this is, but it's a tangible thing and not to be ignored. The nicest thing is that her Aunt Betty doesn't have an evil cell, let alone bone, in her body. She couldn't be any more different from her brother if she tried. Calico Jack is right, Frankie does like his sister. A lot.

Those whose crime was to be business rivals of the Garnet family are herded together in the courtyard. They're to be dealt with individually and returned to *Garnet Cove* a week after they'd been taken. Any recollections of the keep will then be wiped by the vampires. These will be replaced with holiday snaps, fun times and vague memories of too much alcohol.

It's straightforward, but so incredibly boring. Frankie suspects working in banking or insurance would be more exciting in comparison. The one part of the keep enjoying any action is the battlements. Sophie had been so disappointed at not being able to use any of her charges, that Frankie set her a task. Now and then there'll be a loud 'boom' followed by a flash of light as the small witch takes care of the machine guns one-by-one. Selena said there'd been no need for them in her father's time. Her plan is to get back to this style of leadership.

Finally, Frankie has had enough. Not of all the explosions, or the interminable vetting of prisoners. Nope, it's the whining of her grandparents that she's over.

As tempting as it is to make use of a couple of empty prison cells, Frankie wouldn't be able to forgive herself. Family is family, no matter how odious. She's yet to decide what she's going to do about reinstating Calico Jack's powers. It's something she's going to deal with when they're back at *Garnet Cove*.

Frankie clambers up the teetering pile of

wood, steadying herself behind them. Gwen's spell no longer in place it's an easy thing to untie them, at least from the stake. She leaves them roped to each other as this will make it easier for her to keep tabs on them.

A second later and they're standing in front of the large armoire in Selena and William's bathroom. It had been in this enormous piece of furniture that Zane and Frankie had found William on their first visit to the keep. There's plenty of room in there for two with no chance of her being able to hear them down in the courtyard.

Frankie has to use a combination of brute strength and magic to have them sitting back-to-back in the large cabinet. Of interest is that Calico Jack hasn't picked up on Frankie being in possession of his powers. Gwen really has done a number on him, taking every last ounce of his magical abilities.

Their matching expressions of disgust have her laughing as she shuts the door on the ungrateful pair. She's about to turn the key in the lock when there's a flash of light from inside.

"No way!"

Frankie wrenches the doors open, and sure enough, the armoire is once again empty. It's then Frankie spots the runes carved into the inside of one of the doors. As much as she'd like to follow them, she doesn't have time. Neither does she want to be separated from Zane and the others by time and space. Who knew where or even when this particular portal would have her landing? And who's to say she'd even arrive back at the same time as she'd left.

It's a problem for another day. The problem facing her today is keeping a tight rein on Calico Jack's powers. She's managed to control them so far; this isn't to say she can keep it up.

Frankie stands at the end of the dock at *Garnet Cove*. Zane has his arm slung around her shoulder. Dex is lying with his head hanging over the side of the dock. He's checking out the fish that swarm every time he dribbles into the water, on purpose. He hasn't stopped humming since they got back from *All Hallows Keep*.

Zane is nowhere near as relaxed as the small dog. His picking up on the extra powers Frankie has at her disposal has him skittish around her. Like her, he appears torn between her keeping them and giving them back. Not an easy thing with her having no clue where Calico Jack is, or even 'when' for that matter.

They watch as yet another float plane skims across the bay, taking the final group of 'tourists' to the nearest international airport. As plans go, it's been a good one. Their memories wiped courtesy of the vampires, none of the prisoners have any recollection of their incarceration. They'll be able to return to their happy lives and continue as they were.

Frankie almost wishes she could do the same. This has her thinking back on her old life. Would she really want to go back in time to live as things had been before her mom had been killed? While it would be lovely to hug her mom again, this would mean giving up Zane and all her new friends and family.

She also isn't sure how she'd once again handle being powerless apart from her Jeet Kune Do. And anyway, hadn't her mom said she was content on the other side of the veil? Who knows maybe there's a way she can use the Wereall portals to go and simply say hi? Surely that won't mess anything up?

"Well, that's the last of them. I need a holiday after all that mind melding."

Frankie lifts Zane's arm free of her shoulders and turns to find Dominik behind them. She'd been so deep in her thoughts she hadn't even heard his approach. Mind you, the vampires are light on their feet.

Luca and Magda soon join him. While Luca also looks wiped out, Magda is positively bubbling with energy. Frankie suspects the local pig population is snoring loudly courtesy of this. It's interesting that neither Dominik nor Luca has the ability to draw on energy from other living beings. If they don't survive on energy, then what keeps them going?

Frankie looks more closely at Dominik's mouth. It's not hard work. His lips look to have been designed for kissing. He runs his tongue across his bottom lip and warmth pools in her tummy before exploding. She stiffens; aware Zane's also rigid next to her. Unlike him, she's not keeping quiet.

"Was that blood?"

The gorgeous vampire shrugs. "It's the easiest way to control someone's thoughts. And I missed out on lunch."

Luca laughs at Zane and Frankie's reaction to Dominik's snacking on the job. "He's all about multi-tasking is Dominik." That Luca has said this after wiping his own mouth tells of Magda's husband also having had a working lunch.

"It is time for us to leave." Magda steps forward and drags Frankie in for a hug. "I will miss you."

Frankie doesn't like goodbyes. She's had too many in her short life. "Do you have to go?"

Magda sighs as heavily as Frankie has just done. "Yes. We take control of the castle now Natalia is gone."

"Yeah, sorry about that, but she had it coming. You know I left her and Dracul back at *All Hallows Keep*, don't you?"

Magda, while unaware of this, is happy with the outcome.

So is Luca. "We can sleep easy with her out of the way."

"I won't miss that evil piece of work," says Dominik.

Following promises to stay in touch and visit, Magda, Luca and Dominik walk back down the dock. They're meeting up with Sophie in the restaurant. The small witch, while not as powerful as Frankie or Zane, is strong enough to take them back to Transylvania.

Sophie also arranged for Dr Marvin to look after Stanley until such time as Frankie can restore his powers. Actually Sophie wouldn't take no for an answer when it came to getting in touch with the good doctor. Frankie suspects that to stop this from happening would have resulted in a 'medical emergency' of the broken heart variety.

One of the first to leave the island had been Frankie's Aunt Betty. Before disappearing with a mere click of her fingers, she'd hugged Frankie as if her life depended on it.

Frankie's life, that is.

"You simply have to visit me at Hoodoo House. You need better control of your powers if you're to avoid hurting yourself, and others."

This avowal had floored Frankie enough that

by the time she realized she didn't have a clue where Hoodoo House was, it was too late to ask.

Dex having run out of saliva is lying on his back on the dock, enjoying the sun on his belly. *"Does this mean we can go home now?"*

"Not quite buddy."

"Awww, I want to see Marilyn and tell her all about my adventures."

That's right, the piece of canine eye candy from further down Pier 51 back in Seattle. "We won't be here much longer, Dex. We just need to make sure there's no-one from the Garnet family hanging around."

Once they've made sure of this, Frankie and Zane are hitting the whole island with a protection spell. It'll be one that will stop anyone from landing, mostly because the island will literally have disappeared. If their spell goes according to plan, it won't even show up on *Google Earth*.

Only when Zane, Frankie and Dex are alone one the island does Frankie search for any other signs of life. Due to the extra powers at her fingertips, this is as easy as visiting the open space at the top of the island.

There Frankie shuts her eyes and opens her senses. She doesn't hurry the process, wanting to make sure that if Anne and CJ are there that she finds them. She doesn't. They're not anywhere to be found, and neither is the *Jolly Roger*. It looks as if the pair got back to the island safely after all.

They're walking along the beachfront when Nana Peg suddenly appeared out of the cabana on the beach. She's in her human form and dressed in a flowing turquoise shirt and white Capri pants. The outfit suits her figure and coloring perfectly.

She makes a beeline for Frankie, dragging her in for a tight hug. "I'm so pleased I found you."

"I thought you'd be staying with Selena."

It turns out the sisters have been kept apart for years, with Selena a prisoner of the keep as much as any of the inmates. This had been down to it being easier for William to control his wife this way. Frankie's so pleased she locked the horrid man up. No woman needs to be at the beck and call of someone like him.

"Yes, I'm staying with Selena. I just needed to talk to you about something before you leave."

Frankie's stomach drops to her sneakers. She doesn't like the tone her nana is using. It doesn't bode well.

"Do I need to sit down?"

Nana Peg nods in return. Rather than find a seat somewhere nearby, Frankie simply drops to the sand. It doesn't matter where you are, bad news is bad news. She knows this from experience.

Nana Peg drops to the sand next to her, with Zane joining them. He then drags Frankie back is against his chest. Yep, he's picked up that bad news is coming too.

Nana Peg takes a deep breath. "There's something you don't know about being Wereall."

"You mean apart from sprouting fur when I'm under attack?"

"You've experienced this?"

Frankie nods, explaining she noticed it when giving Zane his power back to save him from dying. "Weirdly it was silver, not red."

Nana Peg's eyes widen, although when she realizes Frankie's looking at her, she drops her gaze. Frankie's about to grill her on it, when Nana Peg pats her own silver hair and replies. "Not so strange, really. My fur has remained the same color my entire life. It matters not what color my hair takes when I shape as a human."

"Human?" Frankie wrinkles her nose in concentration.

It's Zane who explains it. "Your red hair comes from Anne Bonny, not the Wereall side of the family."

Nana Peg pats Frankie's arm before continuing. "The first blue moon of the year is coming up. For this you'll need to return to the realm of the Wereall."

Frankie shakes her head before speaking. "Nuh uh, no way. I've survived plenty of full moons with no problems. I am not going back there, like ever."

"And, my dearest granddaughter, how many blue moons have occurred since your jinx was removed?"

"Um, I'm not sure?" Frankie isn't even sure what a blue moon is, never mind when the last one occurred.

Zane knows. "There hasn't been a blue moon since you got your powers back."

"I don't care. I'm not going back to the keep." Frankie jerks free of Zane's embrace and struggles to her feet. There's no way she can sit still when she's this hyped up.

She's joined by the others, although both of them keep their distance.

"Frankie dear, you don't need to travel to the keep. Anywhere away from the human world will suffice."

"Why? What's going to happen if I stay?"

Again, Nana Peg's features are crowded by worry. The news is all bad, like super bad.

Apparently if you're in the human realm when there's a blue moon all heck breaks loose. In summary, you'll find yourself in your animal form with no control over your actions. Last time this happened, over one hundred people were slaughtered. "And eaten," adds Nana Peg with relish, and not the tomato kind.

Her nana's final words have Frankie fighting

the return of her late lunch. She's as keen on steak as the next girl, but not as rare as this appears to have been.

"And my dad, this affects him too, doesn't it?"

Nana Peg nods again. "But don't look upon it as a bad thing. You'll get to meet lots of family you've never met before."

"And I'll be hairy. Like way past due-for-a-wax hairy?" It's strange her dad hasn't made mention of this since getting out of *All Hallows Keep*. Could it be he doesn't even remember? It wouldn't be the first thing he has no memory of.

"Quite possibly, but you'll have control of your animal. Some find it liberating." Nana Peg's broad smile says she's one of them.

Great, here's Frankie thinking she's moving on with life; instead she's stuck joining the petting zoo. Actually, stitch that, it sounds as if she'll be more like something from the carnivore section. Try to pet her and you'll end up losing a hand.

"Yes, well. I'll meet you here two days before the blue moon."

Resigned to her fate, Frankie confirms she'll be there. "Can I bring Dex?"

"Of course, he would be most welcome, as will Zane."

Finally some good news. Even though she'll only be away from home for three or four days, it'll be easier with Zane and Dex along. Of course she'll also have her dad in tow. And that's not something that'll be achieved easily. They'll need to sedate him to travel to *Garnet Cove*, never mind the realm of the Wereall.

Following a quick hug goodbye, Frankie's nana walks down the beach and disappears inside the cabana. Despite knowing she won't be coming out again, it's hard not to keep looking at the little hut. Eventually though Frankie turns and faces Zane. "I need you to remind me of about a couple of things."

"Yeah, sure."

"First off, we're going to have to get some sedatives off Sophie, because we're gonna need them."

"Why, I'm okay with visiting the keep again."

"Yeah, but I doubt my dad will be."

Zane nods his agreement to this. "What's the second thing?"

"When we come back here, I need to pin Nana Peg down on what it was she so conveniently left out about my lineage."

If you enjoyed A SPELL IN PARADISE, I'd be as happy as Dex wolfing down a blueberry muffin if you could leave a review – even a short one. If this is the first you've read in the series, check out the others by clicking here.

THANK YOU

For choosing my book from all those fantastic paranormal cozy mysteries out there! It's readers like you who allow me to pursue my career as a writer.

Lastly, don't be a stranger. I'm mostly online at Twitter, but I'm also on Facebook, Instagram (so many sunset and cat photos) and Pinterest. You'll find all the links on my website.

www.andrenelowauthor.com

ABOUT THE AUTHOR

Andie's love of writing was instilled in her by her mother, although if her mum was still alive, she'd be smacking Andie across the back of the head given the direction some of her writing has taken.

Irreverent, cutting and reflecting her background as a stand-up comic, it's edgy with humor that's a little off-the-wall in places.

Andie lives in the beautiful Hawke's Bay region of New Zealand, an area renowned for stunning scenery and great wine.

Lightning Source UK Ltd.
Milton Keynes UK
UKHW020629280720
367297UK00010B/702